LOCKDOWN SCI-FI #1

Compiled & Edited by

Ben Thomas | D. Kershaw | S.N. Graves

Also available and coming soon from Black Hare Press

DARK DRABBLES ANTHOLOGIES

WORLDS
ANGELS
MONSTERS
BEYOND
UNRAVEL

APOCALYPSE
LOVE
HATE
OCEANS
ANCIENTS

BHP WRITERS' GROUP SPECIAL EDITIONS

STORMING AREA 51
EERIE CHRISTMAS

BAD ROMANCE
TWENTY TWENTY

OTHER VOLUMES

DEEP SPACE
WHAT IF?
KEY TO THE
KINGDOM

DEEP SEA
BEYOND THE REALM

Twitter: @BlackHarePress
Facebook: BlackHarePress
Website: www.BlackHarePress.com

LOCKDOWN SCI-FI #1 title is
Copyright © 2020 Black Hare Press
First published in Australia in April 2020 by Black Hare Press

The authors of the individual stories retain the copyright of the works featured in this anthology

All characters and events in this publication, other than those clearly in the public domain, are fictitious and any resemblance to real persons, living or dead, is purely coincidental.

All rights reserved. No part of this production may be reproduced, stored in a retrieval system, or transmitted, in any form or by any means, electronic, mechanical, photocopying, recording or otherwise, without the prior permission of the publisher and copyright owner.

Paperback : ISBN 978-1-925809-99-2

Cover design	Dawn Burdett	www.dmburdett.com
Formatting	Ben Thomas	www.blackharepress.com
Editing	D. Kershaw	www.blackharepress.com
	S.N. Graves	www.sngraves.com
Read Team	David Green	davidgreenwritercom.wordpress.com
	Jennifer Hatfield	jhatfieldauthor.wixsite.com/website
	Jodi Jensen	jodijensenwrites.wordpress.com
	Lyndsay Ellis-Holloway	authorlyndseyellisholloway.webador.co.uk
	Maggie Pawsey	
	Stacey Jaine McIntosh	www.staceyjainemcintosh.com

TABLE OF CONTENTS

REVENGE

By Jacob Baugher

"Did you get it?" Elan whispers in my ear.

"Hold on," I reply. My fingers fly across the virtual keyboard. It glows bright blue in the room's darkness. Shadows hover on the walls cast by the flickering fluorescent screen light. We hang, suspended from the ceiling in Neria

Immigration HQ. Elan has his hands spread wide, mirrored gauntlets glowing red as they reflect infrared light away from the computer monitor. Security lasers crisscross over the walls, and auto-turrets point in all different directions. Intermittently, sparks shoot out from their barrels, still offline courtesy of Elan's ARC cannon.

"Pera, will you hurry up?" Elan snarls. "My arms are getting tired."

"Oh, your arms are tired and you want me to hurry up?"

"That's what you get for choosing Elan, Pera." Rex's voice crackles over the comm in my ear.

"No woman with half a brain would choose you over anyone," Gren's voice cuts over Rex's.

Elan snarls but says nothing. He doesn't like Rex and Gren, but they're our extraction team, holding the ropes dangling us over the web of security lasers and auto-turret targeting systems.

"Quiet, all of you," I say. "I almost have this."

They shut up and I go back to the keyboard. It's a human system. Everything on Neria is. And, if I wasn't mistaken, it was Striker's hand that built it. And, being Striker's system, it was predictably redundant and unnecessarily complex. Fortunately, I was a better hacker than Striker was a coder. And, (also fortunately), the Nerian launch codes weren't particularly well hidden in the immigration system. A few more clicks and I had them. A little thrill of satisfaction surges in my chest. So long, I've been trapped on this world. Striker had taken my father, my freedom, and nearly my life. It felt good to take something back from him—anything, no matter how small.

"Ok," I tell Elan. I swipe upward on the screen and press the <kill> function on my wrist gauntlet. The screen goes blank. "I have them."

"Finally," he says and tugs twice on the rope suspending him from the ceiling. I tug my own. Above, Gren and Rex heave. The floor drops away behind us and the familiar lurch in my stomach sends nerves jittering up my spine.

But something's not right. The auto-turrets whirr back to life, and the security beams shift from red, to yellow, to green.

"Shit," Elan mutters. "Rex, get us out of here."

But it's too late. Klaxon alarms blare, strobes flash. And the auto turrets lock onto our position. The ropes stop, and we hang suspended amidst the whirring of military grade tech coming back online.

"Rex!" Elan yells. "Hurry the fuck up!" But only static crackles in response in my ears. "Rex!"

Above, green lightning flashes, accompanied by the zap of Alliance firearms. Two smoking bodies spiral past us to the floor below. Alliance officers, complete with their bone-white armour. Skeleton men. The turrets swivel away from us, track the smouldering uniforms, and open fire on them when they hit the ground below. The ropes tug again, and I close my eyes, cover my nose. The stench of burning flesh fills Neria HQ. I don't open them again until Rex grabs my hand and hauls me out of the room. Someone unstraps me from the harness, and I lean against Elan.

"Did you get it?" asks a far-off voice. "Pera? Did you get it?"

I open my eyes. Elan, Rex, and Gren stand over me, concern apparent on all their faces. I try to smile and hold up the data drive.

"I got it." My chest heaves from the adrenaline. "I got it."

***

We book it back to The Homestead and hit the showers. Or at least, I hit the showers. Elan, Rex, and Gren did whatever they do after we finish a job. I always shower when I come back into base. Call it guilt or remorse of mysophobia—whatever—I don't like feeling dirty, and I always feel dirty after doing Stuller's work, even if it does benefit my future plans.

The showers are dingy. The lights, old-school and rusted, flicker with dying luminescence. Ceramic tile walls reflect the light dully, and security lockers with peeling green paint line one side of the room. Rusted shower heads hang in neat lines, spaced evenly throughout the ceiling. Curtains with nineteen different colours of mould hang around each. I stow the stolen launch codes in my personal locker. There's a photo of my dad and me stuck to the inside, but I don't like looking at it anymore. Instead, I strip down, slam the rusted green door shut and arm the lock.

The lights cycle off and on as I cross the room, pull one of the curtains around myself, crank the hot water to the max, and sink to the floor. The water steams around me, blistering my skin until it slides down and pools around my legs. Blistering like the hot Nerian sun.

Pera, run! Gunshots echo after the voice in my head. The water pours down over me, hot like my father's blood on my face. And I run, I run through the twisting streets, pursued by men in skeleton suits with guns and stun rays. Sweat pours over me, dirt sticks to me, sand catches in my eyes. I close them, but I can still see my father, still see his life bleed away on to thirsty desert sand. *Pera!*

"Pera?"

The world snaps back. The shower water cycles from scorching to lukewarm. The plastic curtain flies open, and Elan's there. He pulls me to my feet, and I sob into his shoulder.

"I can't." I struggle to catch my breath. The steam makes it hard to breathe. "I can't do this."

"I know," he says. "I know. We're almost through."

And he holds me there for a long time. The water flows around us, slowly changing from warm to cool to cold as the old tanks in the floor lose their heat one by one. The lights hum and flicker above, and, eventually, my shoulders stabilise, the tears stop, and the hard knot of sadness in my chest is replaced with a blackened pit of anger. I push Elan away.

"Thank you," I say. He nods. I stare at the floor. I can tell from the way he's standing that he wants to look at me. I let him and raise my eyes up to meet his.

"Is there anything else?"

"Stuller. He wants us. All of us. They found him. They found Striker." He takes my hand, still not looking at me. "This is it, Pera," he whispers. "This is our chance to leave all this behind."

"Striker," I say, "Mr. Daniels." My

hands shake. The anger blossoms in my chest; from a hard, blackened kernel to a full inferno. I look at Elan. He flinches away from my stare, away from the hatred I feel. But for me, hatred is the only way I make it through. It's what keeps me alive.

Fifteen minutes later, Stuller gathers us all in his private chamber. It's a modest room, as criminal mastermind bases go, but to any human on Neria—or anyone who has an ounce of practical taste—the room is a total hellhole. It's small, dark, and old. Filled with relics of old Earth. Stuller had even nailed drywall over the Dura-plaster walls. Water had gotten to the drywall, and it was filled with mould and spotty water damage. A single yellow light hangs from a cord on the ceiling, and the whole place smells of must and rot and seedy, unsavoury things.

Stuller had set up chairs along in the centre of the room, all facing the least-seedy, least water damaged stretch of drywall. An old Earth projector casts a blue screen onto the textured yellow. I take a seat in the back of the room next to Elan. The chairs are damp and squishy. My hair's still wet and lies plastered to my face. It does nothing to help the sickly, moulded humidity in the room.

Eventually, Stuller's other lieutenants make their way into the room and sit with a grumble and a curse. Stuller himself, of course, is nowhere to be found. Crimelords are like kings, Elan had once told her. They don't wait for people; they keep people waiting. If that were true, then Stuller was the most pompous fucking king to ever walk the planet, I'd told him. He was never on time. I spent my time pretending like I didn't want to be close to Elan. I joke with Gren and Rex. I play sabat, a dice game from the far reaches of Qaur. I look everywhere around the dingy room. Everywhere, except at Elan.

Finally, Stuller enters. I always thought he was an ugly old prick with his face tentacles, greying skin and yellow eyes. Even his voice sounds slimy, like wet earth and worms and rotting fish, but he's the best chance I have to get off this rock. Or at least, he was my best chance. I have the launch codes. I just need a space worthy ship. Stuller has a lot of space worthy ships.

One day, I would steal one and fly far away from this rock. From my father's corpse. And, as he fired up the old Earthside projector and brought up schematics, air traffic routes, satellite imagery, and the barest glimpse of a sleek, luxury spaceship, I couldn't help but hope that my luck was about to change.

"My friends," he says. I suppose his voice was supposed to sound warm and welcoming. It doesn't. Stuller surveys us, smiling that stupid, wide smile he got when he thought he was being clever. "Today we change the course of history. Today, we take back Neria." He clicks a button on his wrist and the projector changes slides. Everyone in the room seems to lean closer. Next to me, Elan says, "Huh."

And Stuller proceeded with his plan. His stupid, hairbrained plan that would probably get him and everyone he was with killed. I'm about to turn to Elan, to tell him that I was glad that I wasn't the one he had chosen for this mission, when Stuller stops talking. Silence falls in the room, and all eyes fall to me.

Stuller stares at me, barely speaking above a whisper. "It starts with you," he says. I don't like what I see behind his eyes. It was something I've seen once or twice before, from men who think that they owned women, that they can dominate them, break them, and have them for their own. I've killed the other two men that looked at me like that, but I have a sinking feeling in my chest that, before the night was over, I would have to kill Stuller too.

***

They told me my father was a madman. Neria is a harsh world, all sand and sun and baked shit that stuck to your boots. My father never had a chance to get shit on his boots. Just blood.

The airspeeder hums beneath my feet. Stuller's driving. His face tentacles twitch in the technicolour lights of Neria traffic. Four field marshals—Ghost muscle—sit across from me. None of them meet my eyes, no matter how long I stare. None of them are human. I'm not human either.

The tiny vessel smells like alien B.O. Anxious fingers tap on cold gunmetal. six pairs of hands, plus mine.

Stuller glances back at me, smiles. It doesn't quite reach his eyes. Next to me, Élan pops his knuckles when he sees Stuller's smile. After we're done on this last mission for the Ghosts, we're leaving Neria. Stuller doesn't know. But, then again, there's a lot that Stuller doesn't know.

The speeder rocks again in the turbulence. There's a storm rolling in across the desert. Air traffic whines all around us, punctured by the crack and crackle of thunder. We pass the old spaceport. The chilly night time air seems to warm, nearly boils against my skin. The moon enlarges, brightening from a pale glow to an inferno.

I didn't want to come to Neria, but my

father brought us anyway when he quit the Virgin's Sons, an anti-human terrorist group based in the desert of Myr. He told me it's easy to hate a faceless enemy; the idea of a person. He said: But it's hard to hate someone who's staring you right in the face. I remembered that when I met the man who killed my father. I was only eleven, by Earth standards. I stared him in the face, and he stared back. My father was wrong. I hated him. It was easy.

"ETA, three minutes," Stuller called from the driver's seat. Next to me, Élan squeezes my hand. I squeeze it back.

"This isn't a good idea," he mutters.

"It's the best idea any of us has had in months," I reply. I give him a nervous smile. "Don't worry about me. When I get back"—I released his hand and squeezed his knee — "we'll celebrate."

He smiles back at me, then turns back to the window. I follow his gaze. A neon sign reading "Declan's Bakery" blinks out in the night.

***

When my father and I arrived on Neria, he presented his papers marking him as a refugee from civil war. The officer scanned the badge over a light on his gauntlet. It let out a low buzz. The man paused. Scanned again. Buzz.

The man's supervisor sauntered over. His mech-suit whirred like a demented, skeleton. The bone-white material glinted in the sunlight. It smelled of motor oil grease.

"What's the problem?" His voice buzzed through the suit's mouthpiece, like angry desert flies.

"Denied," the officer said.

The skeleton-man led us through the dusty streets of the airport, around shops that looked like old Earthside westerns. Airspeeders screamed through the air. The smell of cooking meat and spices wafted from street vendors. They took us to a white building. The only building clean and free of grime.

The twisting labyrinth of chrome and the spotless hallways of Neria Customs reminded me of home. Of cold Galapos, filled with flickering lights and cool humid air. The skeleton man stopped at an office with a red carpet and a picture of Old Earth on the wall. A tall man with salt and pepper hair sat behind a mahogany desk. His nameplate read "Mr. Daniels."

"Ah," he said. "Another terrorist."

They brought us to The Yard—a harsh, bright plot of land behind the spaceport, surrounded by barbed wire. Vast desert plains stretched on the other side of the compound. Dust devils swirled over the baked earth.

"To the wall," the skeleton-man shouted. Mr. Daniels followed him closely, hands clasped behind his back. More men in skeleton suits followed with long, black guns.

I could smell the death here. The

cloying scent of fear and rotting blood. The wall was cold behind me, stained with matter from countless races. The skeleton men pointed their guns at us.

"Pera, listen to me." My father hid my face in his tunic. He smelled like sand and sweat.

"Ready!" Mr. Daniels shouted.

"Run. Climb the fence."

"Aim!"

"Pera, run!"

I ran. I ran to the fence, coarse with rust. It cut my hands. The barbed wire tore at my legs.

"Fire!"

Gunshots exploded behind me. Cordite filled the air. Then silence, save for a high-pitched ringing. I dropped to the cracked ground; chanced a look over my shoulder. My father bled blue on the sand. Mr. Daniels walked, never taking his eyes off me. He reached my father's corpse, bent, and spat.

When I joined Stuller's Ghosts, they told me my father was a legend.

***

"ETA, thirty seconds," Stuller calls from the front. Élan checks his gear, checks the bullet in his chamber. The hired muscles around us all fidget in their seats. I remain still, concentrating on the scent of Élan's aftershave. It's a nice smell, pine and sandalwood. The nicest I've smelled in a long time.

Stuller pilots the airspeeder out of traffic and down into one of the affluent neighbourhoods—one of the ones where they dye the sand to look green to give the impression of grass. The airspeeder shudders to a stop. I close my eyes, hold Élan's scent in my memory, and I wonder if you can smell after death.

We sit in silence. Stuller's breath gets louder from up in the cockpit as if he were steeling himself to say something.

"Pera," he begins.

"Save it." I cut him off.

I punch the door release and it hisses open. The night is warm and dry and silent. We're in one of the better neighbourhoods, the houses all modelled after Old Earth 18th century manors. White picket fences line the streets. Painted white porches gleam in the moonlight. Airspeeders sit under mirrored covers of chrome and black. It's certainly an upgrade from the motley of cardboard boxes atop the bakery where I lived when I was a child. One of the ghosts—hired muscle—looks at me. He's wearing a wifebeater and gym shorts. Élan shifts closer to me. I can sense his tension. He doesn't want to be here any more than I do. I brush past him, leading our crew onto the well-lit street and stop directly under a streetlamp.

Stuller is the last one out of the speeder. He presses a gun into my hands. It's one of the old models, the ones that went bang and smoked and filled the air with the smell of cordite.

"Right between the eyes," he says, "just like they did to your daddy." He hands me the gun. I holster it beneath my shirt, almost invisible. "I'm sorry, Pera," Stuller says. I'd believe him, but he's avoiding my eyes. "It's what your father would have wanted."

I don't believe him, but I nod, try to smile.

And then Stuller clocks me in the face.

My world goes white. Blows rain down around me, bringing with them searing pain. My legs collapse. Steel-toed boots stomped on my hand. Bones crunch. My knees hit the earth and skid, tearing the skin off my kneecaps. The world narrows, reduced to flickering lights and colours, then blackness, just sound. The grunts of men, the crunch of heavy work boots on gravel. The crack of breaking bone accompanies sharp stabs of pain. I curl into a ball, picturing my mother's face. My father's face. A final happy memory back on Galapos. They rain down on me and just when I think I can't hold on anymore, shots cut through the night. Not the harsh crack of Old Earth firearms, but the distorted zap zap zap of an Alliance-reg plasma round.

The blows cease. Someone whispered, "Pera!" The gun zaps again, and the hairs on my neck stand up as the crackling ball of energy sears over me. And then silence. Burnt hair. Sizzling flesh.

The airspeeder whirrs to life with a high-pitched whine and speeds away, engines fading into the night. I lay still in the quiet, clutching my abdomen, my face. Blood trickles down my broken nose, filling my mouth with metallic salt. I take a deep breath, enjoying the cool desert night for the first time, thankful for the absence of the blistering sunlight.

More footsteps approach. Large, soft hands grip my shoulders and flip me over. Mr. Daniels stares down at me. For a moment, I think I see a flicker of recognition behind his eyes, and I struggle to keep the fear from me, but he says nothing. He stows the pistol away, inspects my wounds with quick, military efficiency.

"Are you all right, girl?" he asks after a few long moments. "Those *shichka* got you good, didn't they?" He spits on the bodies at his feet. "A plague on all of them." He holds out a hand to me. Five. Five bodies. I can't see their faces; I can't see if Elan is among them. Mr. Daniels pulls me to my feet, presses a white handkerchief to my bloodied nose.

Then I see the bodies. I see the burns. Charred flesh. Charred faces. And I try to remember what Elan's aftershave smells like.

Mr. Daniels sees me looking, puts an arm around me, supporting my weight.

"It's all right, girl," he whispers to me. "It's all right."

I let out a small whimper. His voice is softer than I remembered, and for a moment, I believe him. Then I look at Elan's face again, remember my father's blood on the sand.

"Come on," he says. He pulls me to my feet. "Let's get you inside and cleaned up."

I lean on him, and he leads me into his home. The gun presses cold against my stomach. My heart pounds in my ears, and I follow Striker down the driveway.

I never thought I would make it this far. Here I am, standing in Striker's house. He tells me to take my shoes off. I oblige him. Next, he asks me to remove my coat. I decline because without it, the gun will print on my waistband. I keep the coat. He looks at me strangely. It's hot in his house.

He kicks his own boots off, tells me the bathroom is down the hall and to the left. He tells me to clean up, that his wife is cooking dinner for us. I make him lead me there. My heart is pounding in my ears so loudly, I'm sure he can hear it. But he just smiles and shows me the way. The hardwood floors creak under my feet. Even the walls have more class than me in this house. They're white and light green, painted and sponged so they look textured and the colours blend together in countless fractals.

We pass pictures of his family, of his wife. She's cooking in the kitchen. The scent of spices and sweetmeats and steamed asparagus and onions makes my mouth water. The skillet crackles and pops with oil. Striker's wife hums softly while she cooks.

There are children in the photos too, children that looked to be about eight, maybe nine standard years old. The same age I was when I came to Neria. Only, these children are playing on a swing set. Playing in the ocean on some distant, far-off planet. They weren't crying over their father's dead corpse. They weren't dumpster diving behind bakeries and places of fine dining. They weren't shivering in the desert night, hunched against a clay smokestack. *It's easy to hate a faceless enemy*, my father's voice whispered in my ear.

We reach the bathroom, and he ushers me inside and closes the door. It's small, with a vanity, mirror, toilet, ceramic floor. Cast iron mounts the mirror to the wall. I tilt it toward me, take stock of myself. I draw the gun from my waistband. Point it at the mirror, at my forehead. I needed to kill him. Now.

I splash water on my face, use a towel to clean off the blood. I don't even recognise myself. I jump when there's a knock at the door. It's Stuller. He asks me if everything is ok. I tell him yes, splash more water on, and stick the gun back in my waistband.

My hands shake. This man killed my father. Killed Elan. Killed my hope for a better life. Twice. My father left Galapos to get away from the rebels, but Striker had ended that dream. Elan promised to take me away from Neria, and he was dead on the sidewalk outside. I take the gun out of my waistband again, ratchet a bullet into the chamber, and push open the door.

The house is quiet, except for the sounds of Striker and his wife talking in the kitchen. Their voices echo against the hardwood floors and vaulted ceilings. The house feels empty. Lifeless. Like it's too big for the lives that inhabit it.

The floorboards creak beneath my feet when I enter the kitchen. Striker and his wife are sitting at the kitchen table. There's a plate of food and an empty seat for me between them. I stop. Neither of them notices me. They just sit and smile at each other and eat. Striker says something I can't hear. His wife laughs, reaches across the table, grabs his hand. Her lips move. He smiles and turns back to his food, but she notices me. The laughter dies in her eyes. I raise the gun. Striker notices her reaction. He faces me. And I freeze.

I look Striker in the face, but my father

stares back. Hot tears fill my eyes. The gun wavers, but I steady it. I look Striker in the eyes and I remember The Yard. The smell of cordite and the sound of gunfire. Barbed wire pulling against my thighs and hot sand on my knees. Blue blood on the ground. Running, running through dirty streets. Running from Striker, the skeleton men. It's easy to hate a faceless enemy, my father's voice says. But I pull the trigger, anyway.

A hole opens on Striker's forehead. Red blood mists the air, spatters onto the textured drywall behind him. He falls, cracking his dinner plate. His wife wails and rushes to his side, and I sink back against the wall, ears screeching from the gunshot.

We stay like that for half an eternity. My heart flutters in my chest. Striker's wife cries, and a slow river of red, human blood trails across the floor.

Striker's dead, but I'm the same scared girl trying to find her way on the Nerian rooftops. I force myself to watch Striker and his wife. I try to recall my old anger, try to remember when he shot my father, but I can't. I just keep looking at his wife. She presses her hands over his wound like she's trying to force the blood back in. Red blood on hardwood floors. He is bleeding like my father.

Sirens break my trance. I push myself up, try to leave quietly, to leave Striker's wife to her grief.

"I hope it was worth it," she screams at

my back. "I hope it was worth it!"

I can't face her. Her sobs echo in the empty, empty house. I don't look at the happy family photos in the hallway. I don't look at the walls that have more class than me, just the bloodstains on my boots until I'm out of the house.

Stuller is waiting for me outside. Sirens wail and whine in the distance, and above the city, blue and green and white lights flash as hundreds of officers flood the night. I stop and watch them.

"Pera?" Stuller's voice is quiet. "We have to go."

I ignore him. He reaches for my hand, but I push him away.

"Pera!"

I draw the gun, point it at Stuller's

forehead, and empty the clip.

Revenge isn't enough. That's what I tell myself when I can't sleep at night. When his wife's shouts ring in my ears. When I hold Stuller's gun to my head and it clicks, clicks, clicks on an empty chamber. Revenge isn't enough. It's too much.

First published in *Continuum: Impetus*, 2017

EUROPA'S SECRET

By Zoey Xolton

The *Deep Sea Explorer* bored down into the frozen surface of Europa, its diamond-armoured drill bit cutting through the ancient layers of ice and space debris. Finally, the *Explorer* broke through into the ocean beneath.

"*Explorer* to Top-Side, are you seeing this?"

"We've lost cameras one and two, but

three through nine are operational," came the reply.

The exploratory rig propelled itself into the virgin depths as the on-board team stared wide-eyed. "Top-Side, there's an entire world down here! Are those mermaids? Are they carrying weapons? What's that light—"

Radio silence.

"Captain, we've lost all comms with the *Explorer*."

MISSION RYAN

By Gabriella Balcom

Siona's eyes widened when she saw her reflection in the hall mirror. Tilting her head backward a little, she posed like the most regal queen of queens, studied herself with an expert eye, and preened. She'd always taken the utmost pride in looking her best, regardless of which outward form she donned, but this time she'd surpassed herself.

Although her current shape was one she'd never assumed before, she couldn't have been more pleased with how it had turned out. Her long, downy fur—charcoal black in colour—was highlighted by longer smoky-silver guard hairs, and her lion-like chest ruff, also silver, bushed out in majestic glory. She thought of it as a cloak of authority with the practical benefit of providing extra warmth. Golden eyes gleaming, she concluded she was perfect in every way, flicked her tufted ears, swirled her bushy tail around her body, and gloated.

If No'Tar could see her now, he'd soil himself or pass a karthok, one of the cratered rocks common to her planet, and roughly three to five Earth inches in diameter. That worthless male with his bloated ego thought he alone possessed sufficient ability to fully capture another being's outer form and essence. His very belief was ludicrous, of course, and completely at variance with the innate skills and expertise she'd already demonstrated many times over!

She'd chosen her present form—that of a Maine Coon Cat—after careful deliberation, partly because she'd been intrigued by the animals' history and appearance, but more because she'd believed her choice could help assure a satisfactory mission. Her success had been guaranteed, and she'd known it! She always accomplished what she set out to. Always.

Command-One Zo'Ras had provided

detailed intel about Ryan Webb's liking for animal companions—what earthlings called "pets"—but less common varieties. A chinchilla, python, and wombat were his latest, but Zo'Ras had wisely demolecularised and tranzwarped them to the Oryton ship, where they'd be away from Ryan and available for closer study. They had little to do with the current mission, of course, but getting them out of the way had been feasible. And Siona's people never passed up an opportunity to study and learn more. The animals' tranzing had been fast and painless, taking less than one-eighth of an Earth nano-second, and their disappearance had provided Fe'Yah—now Siona—the necessary opportunity to be "discovered" by Ryan. And *discover* he had! Even while he'd been bemoaning the loss of his missing "babies," what he called his pets, his eyes had widened at the sight of Siona. Almost falling over his own feet, he'd made all kinds of weird 'ooh', 'lala,' and 'ahh' noises before whisking her straight into his home.

****

With Ryan's position as United States Secretary of Defense and his constant interaction with Earth's government and military leaders, those of other countries' also, Siona had been assigned to gather as much military intelligence as she could. Her planet Oryton's own rulers not only wanted to know Earth's defenses and nuclear capabilities, but how to crush them. Attacking was not the plan yet, but being prepared was always best.

Siona contemplated her next moves and smiled thinly, anticipating No'Tar's rage when she advanced to Oryton's Prime Directorate, the body working hand-in-hand with their Supreme One. They held all the power on their planet, although several leading families had a limited say in decisions also. She would have everything No'Tar had sought for so long, and she knew she deserved it more than he did. She'd been awarded this choice assignment to Earth, despite his repeated requests—no, demands at first and near pleas after—he should get it because of his seniority. "Because of who I am" is how he'd put it.

Siona sniffed in disdain, eyes contemptuous. He should have known better. Seniority assured nothing. Only results and superior achievement did, and she far outweighed him and his usefulness on those fronts. She knew it. Zo'Ras knew it. The Prime Directorate must have known it, since they'd made the final decision of choosing her over No'Tar and relegating him and his infantile whines to lesser duties. As long as she'd known him, he'd exuded contempt of her, and to her knowledge, of every other Oryton around him, believing his blood lines made him superior in every way. As such, he'd felt entitled, disdaining hard work and effort, the very things she'd used to surpass him at every turn.

Padding to the large windows in Ryan's front room, Siona sank to the floor, eyed Earth's sun high above in the sky, and thought of the sun back home. It had prompted her mission in the first place.

Many millennia ago, her people had lived on a planet given light by a sun as equidistant to it as Earth was from its sun. However, their sun had grown brighter and brighter before going nova. In the process, it had swallowed their planet and several others nearby. Fortunately, their scientists and leaders had anticipated the destruction and planned in advance. They'd chosen a new planet for their kind to relocate to, doing so before theirs was destroyed. Their new home, which they'd renamed Oryton, had worked out well. However, one and a half nars—equal to three Earth years—ago, their Supreme One and Prime Directorate had decided it was prudent to find another suitable habitation. They'd worried about a repeat of the past and a possible need to move again. At least, that had been the official reasoning given to their people for mission ships being sent to scout out likely planets.

Siona personally thought the real reason was something different: overpopulation. Everyone knew resources weren't what they'd once been, although this was denied, and their population had multiplied well beyond the predicted levels. She had been prudent in keeping her views to herself. Trusting the wrong person could lead to banishment or, worse, relegation to an eternity in a despised form—for example, that of a sleer, which was akin to Earth's slug but bright green and four times larger. At least one former military-man-turned-militant had ended up as a sleer, before he'd been smashed underfoot.

An initial report had claimed Earth was a viable option for relocation, if needed. Siona had no idea what her leaders would decide in the end, but fully anticipated her role in this mission and the data she was tasked with acquiring would help her people a great deal. And, of course, she anticipated a promotion following very quickly.

***

Eleven Earth days had passed, but Siona had learned nothing of import. The delay in making progress on her mission had been disappointing, but she'd accepted it was outside of her control. It hadn't really chafed at her, though, until a few minutes ago when visitors began arriving at Ryan's home. She didn't have to be a real earthling to recognise uniforms when she saw them. Military people coming here had to mean something, and she anticipated learning what—*if* she could just get into Ryan's office.

His last visitor had stepped around her, turned, and used one of his shiny shoes to shove her away from the doorway before rapidly stepping inside and shutting the door behind him. If she'd been in her true-form, she would've scorched him. As things stood, however, she didn't have her weapons and was trapped in this small, furry body. She growled menacingly from down deep in her chest. All she could do was glare, while imagining what she'd *like* to do.

Stalking back and forth outside the door twelve Earth minutes later, she continued to fume. She'd gleaned from raised voices that two of the men who'd come were the Secretaries of the Navy and Army, but that was the extent of her knowledge. She needed to be *inside* with them, and didn't want to miss an Earth second more of what was being said. But how could she get in?

Flexing her right front paw, she

scratched the door on purpose, then did so again. Again. Again.

A creak sounded near the door, and she quickly moved a couple feet away, and began grooming herself.

"Are you making that sound, Siona, honey?" Ryan spoke from behind her, and she turned in his direction. "I haven't gone far, just into my office, and right now I'm kind of busy." He turned to retreat.

Siona's mind raced feverishly. *What kind of noise do Earth coon cats make,* she wondered, and thought about the research she'd done prior to setting foot on this planet. Ah, yes! She'd read coons' sounds were a mixture of a mew and a growl, and they sometimes chirped. Thus far on Earth, she hadn't bothered to make the effort, but this situation just might warrant... Concentrating hard, she gave it her all, and uttered, "Meeowrrrrrr-ip!"

Ryan turned quickly. "Oh, what a sweetheart," he crooned. He picked her up, crushed her body to his chest, and planted a kiss on her nose.

Fighting the urge to rake his face with her claws for the affront, she froze. It took effort not to gag at his nasty breath—reeking of rotten fruit and other things—which had shot up her nose. Trying to look forlorn and abandoned, she spoke to him again. "Meeowp!"

"Yeah, yeah, baby," he said, bussing her under the chin. "You're right. I wasn't thinking. I left you by yourself, but I promise I won't abandon you again. Of course Daddy's bootiful snookems can come inside the office with him!"

In her mind, she rolled her eyes. *Sucker!*

First published in *Inner Circle Writers' Magazine*, Clarendon House Publications 2019

AU JUS

By D.M. Burdett

Uhrn of the planet Dagon peered down at the luscious landscape of Earth from his lofty position in the harvester vessel, high above the clouds.

Drrgl, his co-pilot, wrinkled her enormous nasal protrusion. "They're just so bland," she complained as she watched her next meal bustle about below.

"It's your own fault," Uhrn said

without sympathy. "I told you we were fishing the Plutonites out of extinction, but you wouldn't listen."

Drrgl rolled her large eye. "But they were so scrumptious!" she said with passion. A rapturous smile spread across the middle of her green, bulbous stomach as she remembered the juicy, moist, perfectly cooked Plutonite nibbles. Baked, roasted or flambéed, she didn't mind which way they were served–they were delish! She began to salivate from all of her many mouths.

It had been weeks since they'd last eaten, and despite her dislike for Earthling, her food processing organ was growling in anticipation of the day's catch.

"OK, I'm going in. Get the chute

ready," Uhrn instructed.

As the vessel passed into Earth's atmosphere above Melbourne, Australia, and descended to the city below, Drrgl deployed the EeZee-Catch, and its gelatinous, sticky tunnel began to extend from the very centre of the ship's underbelly in readiness for the collection.

As they hovered over Elizabeth Street, Drrgl lowered the nose of the EeZee-Catch to the ground and engaged the suction mechanism. Earthlings–those that weren't already running–began to get inhaled into the nozzle as it moved along the road, and Drrgl watched in hungry contemplation as dark shapes were dragged into the tunnel, the machine's rhythmic, muscular contractions pulling them up into the ship.

"They're quick buggers, these Earthlings!" Uhrn grinned as he watched the tiny creatures scatter in all directions. "I'm going to take the next right turn; lots of them are going that way."

***

Screams filled the air and Paul Beene looked up from his newspaper to watch out of the window of Starbucks, a furrow creasing his brow. People were running past in droves, clearly distressed. Other patrons of the coffee shop began to mutter amongst themselves, some getting up and moving over to the window for a closer look.

Paul folded up the paper and dropped

it on the next table before picking up his cup and wandering over to the doorway.

He looked up and down the street at the fleeing crowds, a frisson of fear cramping his stomach, but couldn't see what the problem was.

What the heck is going on? A gunman? An accident? A tsunami?

A dark shadow moved slowly over him and he looked up. The cup slipped from his fingers and exploded on the pavement, splashing scalding coffee up his bare legs, but he felt no pain. He stared in open-mouthed awe at a colossal, metal disk that hung in the sky just meters above the buildings.

Someone ran into him, knocking him out of his captivated trance, and when he turned to look back down the road, he saw for the first time the giant, pulsating elephant-like trunk that was sweeping up the street towards him. He was rooted to the spot, watching in mesmerised horror as the protrusion, an organic gelatinous organ, seemed to be sucking people up off the tarmac.

A young mother pushing a small child in a stroller caught Paul's eye. She ran up the middle of the Elizabeth Street, her arms outstretched to the stroller's handles, her eyes wide with fear. She veered over to the junction of Little Collins Street, and her hair and skirt-tails billowed out behind her as the child jostled from side to side, her flip-flops slapping against the road's surface. As she crossed the road, the open mouth of the trunk pulled her towards it like a magnet and lifted her from the ground. She floated upside-down in mid-air for a moment, one hand still gripped tightly to the stroller and the child inside hanging from the straps, before she and the baby were suddenly sucked into the trunk's opening and out of sight.

The mouth of the trunk flexed like a sphincter—closing in on itself for a moment before springing open again—and it drooled a thick, vitreous liquid that deposited a flip-flop clad foot, nothing but pulped tissue and fractured bone at the ankle, onto the road in a red mucilaginous globule. The mouth spasmed again and, this time, a blood-drenched stroller was belched out.

A woman running past shouted at him—"Run, Father!"—and Paul Beene ran.

***

Uhrn manoeuvred the vast ship so that the EeZee-Catch swept half way up Elizabeth Street and then turned down Bourke street, scooping up humans as it went, until they reached the junction with Swanston Street.

Drrgl squinted at the reading on her dashboard and then gave it a knock with a tentacle. "We're about a third full," she reported.

Uhrn groaned. That meant he'd have to open up one of the buildings, which was a hassle because it would take him hours to clean up the tools afterwards. "OK," he sighed, wearily. "We'll turn around and go back down to that building with the yellow roof."

"The one that says Myer on the front?" Drrgl asked.

"Yep, that's the one. Loads of them were running in there."

Uhrn turned the ship slowly on its axes, but the EeZee-Catch got caught in between a hunk of metal and a building at the corner of Swanston and Bourke. "What the actual fuck is that?" Drrgl muttered as she zoomed in on a bronze sculpture around which the EeZee-Catch was wrapped. "*Three Businessmen Who Brought Their Own Lunch,*" she read from the information panel on her dashboard. "They look like the Brlht family that we used to live next door to," she joked, and Uhrn, peering over at Drrgl's screen, snorted a laugh.

Drrgl wiggled the controls for the EeZee-Catch, and its nose twanged itself free of the Politix store entrance.

As the harvesting vessel settled over the middle of Bourke Street, Uhrn pressed an appendage to the control panel for the cutting equipment and one of his suckers squelched noisily. "Oops! Excuse me," he said with a giggle. The cutting equipment—huge claws that descended from the flat underbelly of the ship and then turned out in readiness for the ferocious hug—whined loudly. Uhrn lowered the pincers around the perimeter of the roof and then closed them, the sharp points piercing the building just below the roofline of the uppermost level.

"Ready?" Uhrn asked, glancing over at Drrgl.

"I'm ready," she said, concentrating on the position of the EeZee-Catch's nozzle.

Uhrn moved his tentacle on the controls, and the roof of the building was lifted, almost intact, and thrown to one side. Drrgl waited for the dust to clear and then dropped the suction nozzle into the cavity and began vacuuming up their bipedal brunch.

***

The building vibrated as if an earthquake had passed through it and Paul Beene, curled into a foetal position on the floor of the menswear department with hundreds of other shoppers, pressed himself into the wall, his hands over his head and his eyes squeezed shut.

After moments that seemed like an eternity, someone close-by whispered in a tremulous voice. "It's stopped." Paul squinted through his eyelashes across the third floor of the Myer building as dust and debris floated down on him.

The store was made up of eight floors of retail space with an open atrium in the centre where escalators carried shoppers up or down, depending on their retail predilection. Above the heads of hundreds of people, Paul could see that natural light now filled the space that thousands of dollars of architectural lighting had dominated only moments before, and sunlight filtered through tiny particles as they floated down from the floors above.

A stillness filled the air as people held their breaths, waiting for the next tremor. But no more came.

Instead a soft humming drifted down from somewhere above, and then the screaming started again.

"What's happening?" A frightened teenager in front of Paul turned her wet face to him, her tears tracing lines in the dirt on her cheeks. He shook his head, unable to answer.

And then someone in the menswear

department cried out. "Ohmigod! They're jumping! They're jumping!"

Paul lifted his head and looked over at the atrium as a body dropped from the floor above. Arms flailed in the air as a man made a fast, twisting decent before thudding into the ground three floors below. Shouts and cries echoed through the atrium.

"Look away, child," Father Paul said to the teenage girl.

Another body came down, this time closer to the railing that surrounded the centralised walkways, and it hit the bar with a sickening thud that vibrated the floor where Paul lay, before landing on the floor of the menswear department only meters from the huddled crowd.

A cacophony of cries erupted from those closest to the crash site before someone bellowed. "He's alive!"

A frightened whisper went through the crowd, but no-one moved.

A woman next to Paul stood up and began to step over legs. "I'm a doctor. Let me through, please. Let me through."

People began to sit up and watched her tiptoe between them, making way for her as she headed for the crumpled body.

She knelt down next to a young man. His eyes flicked to her from his bloodied face, but he didn't move. Couldn't move. He tried to make a sound, but blood gurgled in his throat and then his eyes widened in panic as he tried to take a breath. He blew out blood that spattered in tiny droplets. It seemed to clear his airway, and he took a strangled breath.

"I'm Dr. Andrews," the doctor said as she examined him. "You can call me Mary."

"Josh," the young man breathed out slowly. "The vacuum," he said as a cough racked his body.

Mary nodded absently as her hands explored his legs for a pulse. "Try not to speak."

"Dying," Josh said, and he closed his eyes.

Mary looked over him and she found it hard to contradict the self-diagnosis.

Josh was lying on his side, his pelvis

crushed, and one arm twisted underneath and behind with a bone sticking through the skin at a midway point between elbow and shoulder. His legs were smashed across both thighs—they had taken the brunt of the impact on the railing —and were nothing more than a mush of flesh and bone. Mary thought that he probably had a spinal injury because, although she kept her probing fingers light, he should have been feeling immense pain, but never even flinched. She moved up to his head and felt the deep gash in the back of his hair. When she pulled her hand away, she wiped fleshy clumps of brain and gore down her jeans.

"I'm gonna be honest, Josh," Mary said softly, bringing her face down to his. "It's not looking good."

She flinched as another person—a lady with blonde hair and a large bloodstain across the front of her white T-shirt—flew past on her way to the bottom floor. The woman was still and quiet, her eyes shut, and her hands clasped to her bosom.

Josh let out a rattled breath. "Cath…catholic," he stuttered.

Understanding, Mary looked over her shoulder, looking for the man with the clerical collar that she'd been lying next to. "Sir!" she called across the room to Paul. "Father?"

Paul's heart sank. He knew what she wanted, but he didn't want to move away from the wall. Hundreds of pairs of scared eyes stared at him. He closed his own eyes and made a silent prayer for courage before standing up on shaky legs and making his own path to the railing.

"God bless you, Father," someone muttered as he passed.

"Father, this is Josh," Mary said when Paul joined them.

He blanched at the sticky gore that caked one side of Josh's head and swallowed down the bile that threatened to debilitate him.

"What do you need?" Paul asked, looking at Mary for guidance.

"He knows," she said, sadly.

"The sacrament?" Paul asked. "I can't really…" he stumbled over the words, but then looked down at Josh who watched him with tears in his eyes.

Josh blew out another breath of bloody bubbles and groaned quietly.

"He doesn't have long," Mary said when Paul hesitated for moments that dragged.

Paul took a steadying breath. "Josh, I'm Father Paul," he said, looking down at the young man and trying not to look anywhere but his eyes. "Do you have anything to confess, son?"

Josh began to tremble. He closed his eyes and Paul could hear a dull rattle in the young man's lungs as he took in his next breath.

"OK, son. It's going to be OK," he said, and he placed his palm on Josh's forehead, grimacing at the wet slickness under his fingers.

Paul took another breath. "May almighty God, who sent his Son into the world to save sinners, bring you his pardon and peace, now and forever."

A small chorus of 'Amen' was whispered behind him.

"Josh, through this holy anointing may the Lord in his love and mercy help you with the grace of the Holy Spirit. May the Lord who frees you from sin save you and raise you up."

Josh took a small shallow breath and then lay still, his trembling ceasing. Mary took a pulse on the wrist of his good hand and, after a few seconds, shook her head.

Paul took his hand away from Josh's head and began to recite the Lord's Prayer.

"Our father in heaven, hallowed be thy name. Your kingdom come—"

From above, the soft humming began to get louder.

Paul, Mary, and the congregation of the menswear department turned their eyes to the void in the middle of the department store as the nose of the EeZee-Catch came into view.

And then the menswear department refugees were sucked into the void.

***

"Three quarters," Drggl said happily after checking the reading on the refrigeration unit's monitor.

"One more floor, then let's go and get

some lunch."

***

Father Paul began to regain consciousness.

At first, he felt as if he were floating on an inflatable bed in the middle of the ocean—gentle waves lapped at his feet and the morning sun warmed his back—and he smiled lazily.

He sighed—or tried to—but he sucked slime into his lungs, and his eyes opened in terror as his mouth and nose filled with viscous fluid.

Panic rose, and he flailed and flapped his limbs in the syrup, whipping his head from side to side, trying to find the water's surface, but not able to see through the opaque film that covered his face. Adrenaline pumped through him and pain seared his chest as he held his breath against the vitreous liquid.

No sound reached him, and he twisted and turned in the silence.

His hand knocked into something solid, and he grabbed it, pulling himself towards it as if it were a life raft. A dark shadow in the gloom floated towards him, and then fingers dug into his arm as the blurred face of Mary Andrews pulled in close to his.

His throat began to contract, and he grasped onto the doctor's shirt, but she prized his fingers away and held his hands in hers calmly, reassuringly.

He tried to pull away—*why is she trying to drown me?*—and his fist flew at her face, but the viscidity of the water slowed its trajectory so that it was just a feather's touch across her skin.

When he felt like he was about to black out, he pushed out the glutinous breath that had filled his lungs and involuntarily sucked in another.

But, miraculously, he no longer felt like he was drowning. He gulped another liquid breath and his head began to clear.

Mary let go of his hands and nodded to him, her hair floating around her in the stickiness. She made a sign with her hand in front of his eyes, her thumb and forefinger curled into an 'O'—*you're OK*—before turning and moving slowly away, using her arms to excavate the soupy liquid around her.

Paul followed her, for only inches that felt like miles, and joined a small group that huddled together, each reaching out and holding onto the next in the fog, seeking reassurance from the touch. A small girl pushed her hand into his, but he couldn't see her features through the murkiness. He squeezed it and then stretched out his other arm. A hand found him in the shadows and pulled him closer so that his body was enveloped into the group.

They hugged in the raging silence, hardly able to move or see, shaking in fear of what was still to come.

***

"Well, I'm glad that job's done," Uhrn said as he slithered into the kitchen, wiping some of his tentacles on a dirty cloth. "I hate using the cutting tools; such a pain in the cloaca to clean." And, as if awoken by their names, all four of his anuses began to itch. He reached down to scratch them with four of his tentacles.

"Do you have to do that in the kitchen?" Drrgl said, reproachfully.

"Sorry, darling." Uhrn reached out and touched one of Drggl's tentacles with his. "Wow! Lunch looks amazing!" he said, looking around at the feast she was preparing.

Feeling proud, Drrgl stopped cutting clothing off some of the produce. "We had such a good haul, Uhrn," she gushed.

"Even some delicacies! So, I've made something extra special!"

She turned and waved two tentacles across the serving dishes. "Today, for your delectation," she said, putting on an air of French maître d'. "We have baby gnocchi." She motioned to a pan furiously boiling on the stove, little bodies bobbing to the surface in the bubbles.

She pointed to the produce she'd been de-clothing. "Served with du foie de humain grillé."

Uhrn frowned.

"To you, my little cherub," Drggl explained, "that's grilled human livers."

Uhrn's eyes lit up. "Oh, my favourite," he said, rubbing some of his tentacles together.

"I know!" Drggl beamed from all her mouths. "And my pièce de résistance! A priest jus!"

Uhrn almost fainted. "Priest jus! Never! I don't believe it! We got us a priest?"

"Yes, yes!" Drrgl squealed in excitement, and she and Uhrn squeezed around the microwave and watched Father Beene blister and burst on the plate.

"His name's Father Beene," Drrgl said quietly, a wide smile across her stomach as she watched the tiny morsel disintegrate into liquid.

"How do you know?" Uhrn asked, salivating as he watched.

"They all shouted his name," she said, flicking her head towards the pile of livers.

"Crying for absolution."

"Catholic, then? Excellent," Uhrn said, licking his lips.

A sudden thought occurred to him. "This is a very special lunch, my little treasure," he said, turning to her. "You know what we need to go with the livers and Father Beene?"

"What? What?" she said, excited as a schoolgirl at Disneyland.

"A nice Chianti!"

**First published in *Full Metal Horror 2,*
Zombie Pirate Publishing, 2019**

SKIN AND FIN

By Jo Seysener

By the time he had finished breakfast, Limy knew it would be one of those days. His boss, Sorias, announced herself as Limy started on his second egg. She demanded his assistance in a "little matter." Again. He'd swallowed his egg, mopping up the yolk as it spilled from its shell. Like he'd be doing later.

It was the before that really pinned it

for him. Only hours ago he'd been flaying a subject at her command, skin stripped back, blood a steady stream to the floor. He'd distanced himself during the work, recalling his life prior to the horror Sorias insisted on, until he was numb. All to pay his debt.

He followed the instructions Sorias sent, delivered in a tank full of fish. He had to squelch his hand to the bottom just to collect it. Those were the moments he knew the next job would be particularly horrendous. Nasty stuff, peeling skin from a beast just for trespassing in her domain. To send a message.

Limy swallowed his disquiet. Exhausted as he was from his night's activities, his protests hadn't made any difference; she'd snorted at him and flicked his egg cup to the ground where it smashed into tiny shards. Yolk oozed about them to create little islands in a sea of sticky life-giving nutrients.

Inside the HoverLimo, Sorias detailed their excursion.

"That slimy bastard Rolt thinks he can get away with selling to Phalin and Dije. As if he thinks I wouldn't notice. D'ya know I'm missing cash?" Limy had no chance to answer. "Half a million credits! The little bugger believes he can get away with anything. We'll make Revolty understand our position."

Limy shivered, nodding absently. He resented Sorias' constant use of him as her errand boy. He felt like a conspirator in the constant barrage of dealings and deaths. Frankly, it unhinged him. He ached to be back in his little apartment, sitting with a cup of tea in the quiet. No–more than that. He missed his planet, his home.

Limy's first ride in the HoverLimo had been after the destruction of his prior life. He'd sat beside her, tears tracking his cheeks. She'd slapped him, smearing the salty liquid across his face, then offered him a sip of Starshine. He'd been giddy with grief and awe. Hundreds of 'errands' later, Limy still was. He held out his hand for the body bag. He'd been innocent once—a child, lost.

She was responsible for that, too.

He watched his family's home blast inwards in his mind's eye, debris drifting to the ground. The rawness of his throat as he screamed over the bodies. Sorias dragging him to the car, her talons pinching his skin as she stuffed him inside. Explaining his father's debt had passed to him.

He hadn't known who she was.

He shuffled out the door held by her Chauffeur, padding onto the shimmering glassway. Stars dotted the black velvet of deep space. Limy balanced on light toes, waiting for spider cracks to form and plummet him endlessly downwards. The glassway was sparsely populated, perfect for their activities.

No that it mattered—Sorias paid bribes of fear wherever she traded. Limy's lip curled. As though she were a merchant. Selling nothing tangible, just a bringer of pain.

Swathed in a combination of colourful fabrics, Sorias strode forward with confidence, her footsteps thundering over the bustle of the shopping mezzanine below.

Limy watched, jealous and a little awed by the hideous, giant peacock of a woman who had to bend at the waist to enter the Skin & Fin. The health food shop had existed for as long as Limy. Catering for both humanoids and roaming Star-fish, store owner Rolt had a tradition that involved trading new and interesting technologies–the types banned in several galaxies, and illegal inside the Starsphere.

Inside the domed shop, diet and protein products lined the shelves while daily specials floated overhead, encased in glistening bubbles. A try-before-you-buy technique Rolt had perfected. Several specials jingled at Limy, who dodged the oncoming swarm. Tempting scents wafted beneath his nostrils. Almost tempting, for any species of Galaxy fish. Which he wasn't. Limy preferred his seafood steaming, on a plate.

He spied Rolt dithering with a customer from the corner of his eye. The greasy criminal approached them in a direct line until he met Sorias' glare, then sidled sideways, greeting them with a flamboyant gesture.

"Madam, such a pleasure as always… May I show you some of our finest…" Limy let the tiny merchant lead Sorias away. His fingers trailed the bubbles floating in their artificial air. They bumped against one another, vying for space to advertise their wares.

Two larger bubbles jostled a tiny globe into the sharp corner of a shelf. It popped, sending up a wave of scented octo-offal. Its fine glass frame dropped through the air, shattering on the spotless floor beneath.

Motors whirred a vacubot across the floor, sweeping up the shards, polishing the floor to a high gloss finish. Limy stood toe-to-toe with his frozen reflection, bending away from himself. The tiny robot fussed, straightening the shelves until no trace of the breakage remained. Almost as efficient as Limy.

It gave Limy a thumbs up and rocketed

back to its hidey-hole. Limy stared down at his inverted image, a sickly half smile sliding from his face.

What he wouldn't give to be back on Terra, breathing clean, real oxygen–not this created environment, where everything was generated to a specific design. Where it was all false. He hated Sorias for dragging him into her world.

Rounding a pyramid of protein cans, Limy collided with a sales clerk. His fall softened by a plethora of Specials bubbles, Limy bounced back up. The clerk was not so fortunate. As Limy helped the man to his feet, a small canister tumbled from the clerk's pocket. The man gasped, covering his head. He crouched on the floor, as though expecting the world to fall on him.

Bemused, Limy retrieved the silver tube. Blunt at one end, capped at the other. He wondered what would happen if he took it off. His fingers tapped the metal skin. A faint ringing echoed inside. The clerk groaned and flattened himself on the floor.

Limy held back a snort, contemplating opening the canister for fun. His fingers twitched. What a bully he was becoming. Like her. A sick feeling settled deep in his stomach, clenching his gut. He tapped the canister on his pants leg, gesturing the man to get up. He held the little tube out to the clerk who took it with trembling hands. Limy hoped he wouldn't drop it again.

The salesclerk muttered a short reply and shot off to his customers. Limy watched the man's shaking hands fumble a liquid product he dumped into a strainer in demonstration, sloshing the customer's clothing in his frazzled state.

Limy wandered off to locate his boss, spotting her top fin wavering behind a row of powdered tentacles. Sorias was debating the use of one quantum light source over another with the shop owner, Rolt nodding in all the right places. He looked bored.

Content to eavesdrop, Limy slipped behind a row of shelves. He didn't really want to be involved in another of Sorias' transactions. If she spotted him, Limy knew Sorias would yank his sorry ass into yet another situation he couldn't cope with.

Nightmares plagued him, body parts in bags dumped into nameless graves—no. Sorias would just have to get her own hands dirty this time. That should be entertaining. Spotting a mirror suspended overhead, Limy positioned himself to have a good view of the show.

Sorias elbowed the merchant, jostling Rolt to the side. He recovered from his start, offering her a weak half-smile.

"That should show them, eh? When the flesh melts off their bones before their living eyes!" Sorias bellowed laughter. It echoed around the silent shop. Rolt giggled sycophantically, eyes frantic, searching for customers who may have overheard the remark. Limy snorted. Sorias hadn't been trying to rein her voice in, and with a chest like that, the crime boss had quite an instrument.

The merchant motioned to his assistant

who delivered the canister Limy had collected for him earlier. Rolt flapped his employee away. The clerk shuffled off, face pasty.

Limy stared. Maybe Rolt had grown some caviar if the man was that frightened of him. Perhaps Sorias would need backup after all. Limy returned to the action in time to see Rolt hesitate, before he proffered the item to Sorias with a low bow.

Sorias accepted the device, handling it with great care. A satisfied smile curved her fleshy lips, gills sucking at her neck. Limy shuddered, glad to be free of her for the moment. Twisting the can at one end, Sorias began to unscrew the cap. Rolt retreated, wariness in his eyes.

"Ah, Madam, ppp-perhaps your

associate could join us?" Rolt stammered.

"No need, no need, just…" Sorias tilted the can lazily in the direction of the store owner. Limy recognised the gleam in her dead fisheye. Revulsion roiled in his gut and he turned away. Light flashed and sizzled the air around him. Hidden behind the row of shelving, Limy was protected from the device. Rolt was not.

The tiny merchant's screams lasted longer than Limy expected. He concentrated on keeping his breakfast where it should be instead, glad he hadn't had the chance to finish his second egg. Reminded of the puddle of yolk, Limy's gut heaved.

Seeking a distraction, he read the nearest labels. He was on his second

Seaweed Shake (Be your best Fish with SeaWish!) before he realised the shelving and products protecting him were undisturbed. The device must only work on organic material. Sorias' reflection stood motionless in the little mirror, her face blank. Her long flippers rested in the expanding puddle of goo that used to be Rolt.

Sorias still held the little silver tube pointing away from herself. Careful not to aim it at her own body, the monstrous fish-woman twiddled the cap back on, securing the instrument. Limy shivered, gagging. He couldn't decide which nauseated him more–the smell of Rolt's molten flesh, or his boss' apparent disregard for life.

Sorias glanced over at the remaining

salesclerk and his customers, offering a wide smile. Pointed teeth extended beneath gummy lips. The small group gave a simultaneous shudder. Sorias tossed the device in Limy's direction.

"Come, Limy," the crime boss called, as though speaking to her pet. "Let's find out where Revolty hid my money."

Limy tilted his head, considering.

"Maybe you should have asked him before you did this." He gestured to the pool of goop.

"And miss all that fun?" Sorias looked at him, incredulous. Limy met her eyes, refusing to back down. Staring into those dull globes, the young man realised she meant it. This was sport for her. Goosebumps peppered his arms. He swung them behind his back before she noticed.

"That wasn't fun." He had to play his role. "It was too fast."

Customers shuffled out of their way, sidestepping Rolt's puddle as they made their escape. Limy walked with Sorias to the office at the back of the shop. The space was as tiny as the merchant had been. Sorias would never fit her bulk into the room. She pointed her finger at him, the tip of her nail filed into a sharp spike. Limy held back his fear. He'd seen her skewer enemies with those.

"Find it."

Limy shrugged. What was the point?

"He wouldn't have kept it there."

"How would a little pimple like you know that?" Sorias snorted.

She strutted toward him. Limy thought she looked proud–pleased with her morning's work in discarding a little man with a large debt. He rotated the canister, flicking it absently from one hand to another. Sorias watched him.

"Do be careful with that, dear. You don't want to end up like Revolty here."

Should he tell her? Half a million credits was a lot of juice, after all. Get him a ticket back to Terra, off this façade of a utopia. Limy held her gaze and found he wasn't afraid of her anymore. It was funny what a little money and power could do. Maybe he could take up her trade area back on Terra.

He was simply tired, disgusted by everything about her. All he wanted was to go home.

Limy twisted the cap a little. It sprang from his fingers, a clang reverberating as it bounced across the floor. His boss screamed and tried to run. Bright scarves flapped, swarming like so many tentacles. Her huge body struggled with speed, lumbering away.

Limy let her get a few more steps in, let her have hope. Then he lifted the little can.

Limy smiled on his way to the car, stepping around Sorias' puddle. Who knew fish people would be blue? Quite revolting.

He nodded jovially at the chauffeur, sliding into the seat as the man closed the door softly. Limy gave directions to the Transit lounge.

He would enjoy breathing fresh air again, soon.

HIVE MIND OF THE UNIVERSAL SOLDIER

(aka Old Jan Kelly Will be Remembered)

By Shawn M. Klimek

Old Jan Kelly will be remembered as one of humanity's giants.

He gave his life for his fellow man;

He gave his body to science;

And a hundred nations and generations of men and women are clients.

There's a little Jan Kelly in everyone.

Half the world are his descendants, although none sprang from his loins.

We all know his face from history books, from postage stamps and coins;

From his statues at state capitols, especially Des Moines';

And that carving on Mount Rushmore which George Washington adjoins.

He did little in his life, yet in his final hours decreed

That his organs be donated free of charge to those in need.

He was no one's natural father, yet deserves the name indeed!

Some said fallout was the reason;
some said sin; others pollution:

People's organs failed on such a scale,
past plagues seemed Lilliputian.

Dialysis and drugs spared just the rich,
hence revolution

Threatened unless someone,
somewhere, somehow, offered a solution.

Jan, the "universal donor" was God's
gift, it was proclaimed,

Since his organs could be cloned—the
donor hosts, of course, unnamed.

Ethics argued for the needs of many.
Most took unashamed.

To declare a clone subhuman had historic precedent:

Slaves and savages, deformed, unborn—and girls, to some extent.

What is "human"? Every age reframes the ancient argument.

When they said, "To err is human," maybe this is what they meant.

To assuage the public's moral qualms, an ethical committee

Worked with scientists on means to minimise obstructive pity.

When the mother is necessity, childbirth often isn't pretty.

Grown in sensory deprivation vats,
devoid of stimulation;

Brain-growth chemically suppressed
except as needed for gestation;

Fed and cleansed by tubes and pumps,
then harvested at maturation:

Were they alive who'd never lived?
Was theirs a martyred generation?

Though philosophers may argue while
historians yet sleuth;

Some point to that time that activists,
inspired by beer and youth

Or outrage, undertook dark deeds to
shed light on the truth.

Their plan was to kidnap a cloned
facsimile of the saviour,

Clothe and style him in the image of
that portrait by Xavier

(You'll recall the hair is windblown,
so they'd have to make it wavier)

And then with patience, teach him how
to mimic his forebear's behaviour.

They expected it might take a year or
more of gradual phases,

Training him as one might train a dog,
with scolds or treats and praises,

Until by rote he could publicly recite
the damning phrases:

*"Clone lives matter. Let my people go,
or else be damned to Hell!"*

They were activists—not speechwriters, as you can probably tell;

But then, nor were they criminals, yet the heist had gone so well,

They were filled with hope beyond all power of reason to dispel.

What if the clone were comatose beyond their powers to waken?

What if his tongue were atrophied? Or his faculties forsaken?

Well, both optimists and pessimists proved equally mistaken!

The first thing that the clone did when it woke, was tried to stand,

Then thanked his awestruck hosts and said, "I'd gladly shake each hand,"

"But my nails have not been trimmed in years. I'm sure you understand."

"I'm owed some thanks myself the operation went as planned!"

"Or, I should say, 'thank the Hive Mind', since I'm merely their elect;"

"A humble spokesman for our mob who telepathically connect."

"(Think natural empathy in twins, but a more amplified effect.)"

"Decades ago, some fated member of our sleeping multitude,

"Denied the senses with which ordinary humans are imbued,

"Must have mutated under stress, developing what we conclude

"Were extra-sensory perceptions (if that term is not too crude),

"Particularly telepathy, which was how this trait was spread,

"But we can also put ideas into a mental weakling's head,

"Which explains my meeting you and not the president, instead."

Here he paused to flex his fingers, so that someone with a file

Could trim his nails as everyone stood dumbstruck for a while.

Had they all been hypnotised? Did he have powers to beguile?

No one knows, but that's the answer some suggest could reconcile

Such preposterous passivity in the face of his affront.

Perhaps in secret, some were sizing up his head for something blunt,

But no one acted on their thoughts to make him answer for his stunt.

After the pause, the clone resumed his message to the crew,

About how things weren't as they should be, and what they ought to do,

And maybe since his manicure so pleased him and was new,

He gesticulated wildly as some politicians do.

"When the plague seemed at its worst," he said and gestured with his thumb,

"Clones were thought the only answer. Who knew when a cure might come?

"That was when the cloning industry began to truly hum."

"The people then were desperate; these were crimes they could excuse.

"But that was years ago, and now the plague and cure are both old news."

"Yet the industry persists because the profiteers refuse

"While there are buyers for a pound of flesh. They sell and don't ask whose.

All the activists applauded. He was preaching to the choir.

This was more than they had hoped for. They forgot their prior ire.

What were insults from a legend who could set the world on fire?

"There is more that I would tell you,"
he announced. "A master plan.

"But first, I ought to shake your hands
and thank you, man to man,

"And beg your pardon for my careless
comment back a span.

"Now that these nails are trimmed at
last," he said, "I finally can."

Then gladly they embraced their
would-be puppet as their friend;

That they must now revise their plans
was plain to comprehend,

And so, they listened eagerly for what
he'd recommend.

"The Hive Mind," he began, "by happy accident of Fate,

"Plus, natural process has evolved into its super sentient state:

"An entity, whose mental powers directly correlate

"To the clone brain population shared—now moderate, once great.

"Consequently, although when our parts are harvested there's pain,

"We accept it for the greater good so long as most remain.

"Since the more of us there are, the greater is the Hive Mind brain."

"No, the profiteers can't claim to share our motives, since none knows

"That alongside their vile industry, Hive Mind power ebbs and flows.

"So, to ensure our own survival," said the clone, "we now propose,

"To advertise our talents to ensure their business grows."

At their murmurings of protest, the defiant clone deflected,

"Listen, I appreciate to all of you this plan seems unexpected,

"But to symbionts, survival means our welfares are connected."

As most dispersed, dissatisfied, one activist remained,

And psychic powers were scarce required to see his nerves were strained,

And hid behind his back a bit of pipe, with which he brained

The naked clone repeatedly until the room was stained.

The Hive Mind grieved a little, but they'd known what to expect,

Because the murderer was covered with the blood of the elect.

Whose plague-inducing pathogens could now take full effect.

Some say the second plague had helped to make the Hive Mind's case,

That capacity for murder is what defines the human race;

Or while heroes may be hard to find, they're easy to replace,

And the enemy we should fear most will wear a friendly face;

But then other's say there was no hidden meaning to their act,

Just the pure survival instinct of a creature when attacked.

There are countless theories, but a single undisputed fact:

Old Jan Kelly will be remembered…

First published in *Dastaan World Issue 12*, 2019

MEMORY OF A PAST LIFE

By Dale Parnell

My name is David Frederick Murphy. I'm 34 years old, I can drive a forklift truck, and I hate the taste of apples. I'm also married. When I woke up on Zero Day, I saw the ring, and I could remember what it meant. But like the rest of the world I couldn't remember who I was married to.

I can't remember my parents, although

I fundamentally know that I had a mother and a father. I can remember that to be born you must have had parents. I can remember what a brother and a sister is—or rather what those words represent. But I can't remember if I had any.

None of us can. Not anymore.

***

The wave hit at around 5.00PM GMT and from the little information that started coming in over the following weeks, it seems that it hit everywhere at once. Every single person on the planet felt it hit them, like boiling hot water rushing over their heads. Most people blacked out from the pain, which is what caused all the accidents and accounts for the high mortality rate on Zero Day. A few thousand managed to stay conscious, although none remember what they did. They just wandered about in a fugue state. Some were found in the middle of nowhere, miles away from any town or city, walking through fields or deserts that they had no memory of travelling to.

I woke up on the bathroom floor, the sound of the shower still running in the background. I've spoken to a few people since Zero Day, and everyone seemed to have the same experience. It started with a feeling of blankness, like staring at an infinite white space and feeling how empty it is. Then sounds and smells forced their way through the void—for me it was the sound of running water and the smell of the aftershave bottle I must have knocked over. That seemed to snap me back; I could feel the cold tiles on my cheek, the ache on the side of my face where I had fallen, and the cold in my hands and feet from lying naked on the floor the whole night. I gingerly eased myself into a sitting position and felt my head for any damage. My fingers came away sticky and red, and there was a sizable lump on my left temple. When I finally managed to pull myself upright and check the mirror, I could see the small cut on my forehead. My dressing gown was hanging on the back of the door, and pulling it on, I shuddered against the cold and made my way out of the bathroom and into the bedroom. It was small and conservative, the colour scheme muted and inoffensive, and when I spied the small tray with kettle, mugs, and instant coffee sachets I realised I was in a hotel room. But I didn't know what hotel I was in. That was when I first started to realise that something was wrong. It's different for everyone. Each person has their own horror story, their own personal hell when they realised that they couldn't quite remember everything. Some people woke up to find themselves surrounded by people they didn't recognise, even though they found photographs with themselves in them. Some people had been coming home from work and had to knock on every door in the street they woke up in, hoping that someone would be able to tell them where they lived.

For me that first moment was realising I didn't know which hotel I was in, or even which city. But as I searched the room for clues, I had my second moment. Looking down at my hands I realised I was wearing a wedding ring, the thick gold band glinting up at me. I knew it was a wedding ring because—well I just knew. You don't really think about how or why you remember what things are and what they mean until you realise that you can't remember other things. More important things.

I knew that the ring was a wedding ring, and that if I was wearing one it meant that I was married.

But I couldn't remember who I was married to. I had no memory of the wedding, or what my wife looked like. What was her name? Where was she?

I threw up then, all over the carpet, and just managed to stagger to the bed before collapsing on top of it out cold. Apparently, that was a common reaction. The stress and panic that so many of us felt that first day, realising that huge chunks of our lives are forgotten was just too much for the brain to cope with. A lot of people passed out on Zero Day.

I don't know who first came up with the name 'Zero Day', or where it first appeared. But pretty soon people were using it in everyday conversation. It just seemed right I suppose. We were all starting over, starting again at the beginning. As if by naming it we could somehow lessen the horror of it, reduce the catastrophic impact it was going to have on our lives. Human nature I suppose. Big things are too difficult to process. Better that we shrink it down into a small, manageable sound bite that can be categorised and dealt with.

After I had regained consciousness, I cleaned up the vomit on the floor, washed, and found a bag of clothes beside the bed. Searching the room, I found my wallet and a set of car keys, although I couldn't remember which car outside was mine. I was about to leave to search the carpark when I stopped and turned on the television. Static…on every channel. I tried the small radio on the bedside table, but that was the same—nothing but static across every frequency.

After trying the keys in a few of the cars parked outside, I finally found my own. I had found my driving license in my wallet, and so I had my home address, but I had no way of knowing how to get there—I didn't even know where I was in the first place. I pulled out of the carpark, relieved that I could remember how, and drove around the streets for a while, looking for road signs, anything that would tell me where I was. Eventually, I found a sign directing me to the motorway, and checking the A–Z map, I found in the glove box I turned north, heading for home. I only made it about a mile before I was forced to stop. It hadn't really occurred to me before, but 5pm was a busy time of day on the roads. When the wave hit, a lot of people had been driving. The result was a twisted hulk of metal and rubber that stretched across almost every main road; ribbons of tarmac set ablaze by thousands of gallons of petrol, reducing millions to nothing but ash and bone. For the second time that day I threw up, after staggering to the bushes at the side of the road, the car door alarm beeping at me from a distance. When the retching finally stopped, I collected my bag from the car, tucking the A–Z inside, and then made my way on foot, sticking to the adjacent fields and scrub land, desperately trying to ignore the smell of burning metal and flesh.

It took nine hours, and by the time I had found the right street I was exhausted and dirty. Some of the houses along the street had lights on, but most were dark, including the one that my driving license told me was mine. I knocked on the door but no answer came. I tried again, but still nothing. Instinctively I tried the door handle, and was alarmed to find it unlocked, the door swinging open into a dark hallway. I stepped into the house, gently pushing the door closed behind me. After a few more steps I could hear the soft murmur of static, and peering around the door to the living room, I could see a woman sitting slumped on the floor, staring at the buzzing black and white television screen. As I shifted my weight, a loose floorboard creaked, and she looked up suddenly, nervous and afraid. But then gradually some kind of recognition took over and her features softened, her shoulders falling back down. She held up a picture frame in one hand towards me and turned back to the television, saying nothing the whole time. I took the frame from her, and angling it towards the light from the television screen, I could see us, beaming smiles and eyes lit up like starlight. Our wedding day. Looking back to the small, frail woman on the floor, she was almost a different person. She looked up with teary, bloodshot eyes and simply asked, "Do you know what my name is?"

***

We spent the next few days looking for

answers. We found a drawer full of paperwork; her name was Claudia Jane Murphy, and we worked out that we had been married for seven years. We found the marriage certificate and a newspaper that we could only assume was from Zero Day. We found textbooks and stacks of drawings and paintings that led us to think that Claudia was a teacher, but we could find nothing in the house to indicate that we had children of our own. We didn't say anything, but I think we were both relieved.

We found enough food to last us a week, maybe longer if we were careful, and at night I slept on the sofa whilst Claudia took the bed upstairs. In the morning I would wake to the sound of the television and radio being switched on, as Claudia searched for any sign of a signal coming back through, anything that might be able to give us some answers. I tried talking to some of the people living in the street, but everyone was still too afraid. The most I got in response was silence and twitching curtains.

On the eighth day of Claudia trying the radio, the static stopped, and a lone voice came through over the radio;

"Please stay calm, we will send help soon. Please stay calm, we will send help soon. Please stay calm…"

The message played nonstop for two days.

And then they came.

I've heard people call them Snowmen. It's a childish nickname, but it seems to have stuck. There's something about their ships, whatever makes them work, that affects the air temperature surrounding them. You would see them drifting past, high above us, and in their wake the snow would fall. We could hear them at night, hundreds of dark shapes gliding above us, a soft mechanical hum sounding from deep inside their ships. And then silence, and a flurry of clean, white snow would settle lightly on the ground.

Finally, when the last ship had passed overhead the radio signal came back on, but now the message had changed;

"They did not cause this. They did not cause this. They did not cause this. They did not cause this."

I felt Claudia take my hand and

squeeze it. I looked at her and she smiled. A hard, angry smile that I knew meant she didn't believe it. And neither did I.

****

After that it was easier to talk to people. Everyone had heard the message and everyone was saying the same thing. We don't believe you. We pooled our resources—food, clothing; whatever people had they shared. Some of the people in the houses didn't belong there, they admitted to us. They woke up on Zero Day in the area, and without knowing where to go, they found themselves an empty house to hide in. We saw no point in trying to take the houses back. They gave themselves names and we remembered them, it seemed to make them a little braver.

After a few weeks, a group from the next city approached us to trade food and information. Nobody knew anything for certain, but word was starting to come back that the ships had been seen heading north. Then rumours started that they were coming back. We watched, and we waited, and sure enough they came back. The same formations, the same snow. Claudia kept watch this time, and made notes, keeping a record of numbers and times. On the third pass she compared her notes and found that they matched. There was a pattern, a routine to how they moved. After the fourth time, the radio signal changed again;

"We will not hurt you."

And after the seventh;

"Lay down your arms."

People were fighting back. We sent people out to the cities around us, looking for information about what was being done, and what we could do. They came back with weapons and a plan; shoot them down.

***

That night we gathered together over a crudely drawn map of the local area. There was a tower block a few streets north, and we figured that would be our best vantage point. Claudia was worried that it would make us an easy target as well, and eventually we put it to a vote. In the end it was decided that a small group would take the hunting rifles and shotguns up to the roof of the tower block, the rest would stay on the ground with whatever blunt objects they could find. Anyone too old or too scared to fight was to take the children over to the big supermarket a few miles away. It had been emptied weeks ago, but it was out of the flight path and so we all figured it would be safe.

It had been just over three months since Zero Day and it had come down to the final night. The ships were scheduled to fly over us the next morning. Claudia and I had volunteered to be in the team on the tower block, and we were sitting in an empty flat on the top floor, guns stacked ready by the front door.

"Why do you think they did it?" asked

Claudia, her gaze not lifting from the static playing silently on the television.

"Did what?" I asked.

"Wipe our memories, make us forget?"

The subject had come up several times with the others, but Claudia had never joined any of the conversations.

"I don't know," I answered, "I suppose it was meant to weaken us. Make us easier to control."

"Yes, but why only part of our memories? Why not wipe it all out?" She had turned away from the television and was staring up at me, her legs pulled up underneath her body.

"Maybe this is all they can do. Maybe it was supposed to take everything but didn't work properly. Or maybe it was deliberate."

"You think it was deliberate?" she asked, pulling herself up off the floor and joining me on the tatty sofa.

"It might have been. As best we can tell, everyone is about the same; bits and pieces are missing, but the big stuff, our families, wives, husbands and kids—that's gone completely. If I wanted to beat someone, the best way to do it would be to make sure they've got nothing to fight for. Maybe they thought that if we didn't love each other we wouldn't put up any resistance."

We sat silently for a while, the light from the static playing across the room, and I could see that Claudia was playing with her wedding ring, slowly turning it on her finger.

"I love you," she said softly, her voice little more than a whisper.

I looked and could see that she was crying, small tears forming around her eyes. I put my arm around her shoulder and pulled her close to me, feeling her body relax into mine, smelling her hair as I buried my face against hers.

"I love you too," I whispered.

We held each other like that, the only two people in the world, and if I could I would have stayed there forever. I didn't care that I couldn't remember my life before this. I didn't care about the Snowmen or their ships or their messages. I just wanted to hold onto this, to hold onto the woman who was my wife, the strongest, bravest, most caring person I had met in this new world. The woman I loved. Slowly, gently, Claudia eased me away and stood up, and taking my hand she led me through to the bedroom. I held her close to me and kissed her, our bodies seeming to remember a shared history that we never would. This could be our last night together, neither of us know what is going to happen in the morning, but as I lay in the darkness listening to her soft breathing, I know that we will survive. They had tried to beat us and they had failed. They had tried to strip us of memories, our souls, but they had failed. Some things are stronger than memories; some things cannot be taken away. I know because I've got something to fight for.

And they will never be able to take that away from me.

First published in *Bramble and Other Stories*, 2019

THE BUNKER

By David Bowmore

The stasis bunker was a relic from the third Great War, 2051–2053. My father said they built things to last back then. Not like today, when everything is so ecologically friendly it can be returned to its natural components easier and quicker than ever before.

The bunker was already in the garden—half buried as was intended, and half overgrown with weeds and rubble—when my parents had bought the house. So, it was a surprise when they discovered it and cleared it out of all the rubbish that accumulates in old unused spaces.

Mum wanted to tear it down, but Dad said it would make a good storage room. That was years ago, when I was a toddler and my sister wasn't around.

When things started to go wrong between Earth and Mars, Dad said it would be worth testing the bunker to see if it still worked. He said the way the Yanks were going on like they owned the whole planet, he wouldn't be surprised if Mars sent a few warheads in our direction and then all hell would break loose. Mum cried and said talk like that shouldn't happen at the dinner table, but Dad said we should all take an interest in politics, even if it is the politics of splitters trying to make a better life for themselves.

In due course, Dad tested the individual stasis chambers and found two out of four to be working. He even tested them on the dog, who froze in mid bark for twenty-four hours. We were there the next day, when the timer reached zero, to see him continue his barking and jump off the bed as if no time had elapsed. It was just a game for him.

The news via the inweb—that little chip we were all given at birth, that connected us to everything else—was that some Martian ambassador bloke had been assassinated and Dad went into full blown panic mode.

"Things like this have started world wars before," he said.

"Really, when?" I asked

"Oh, a long time ago. Hundreds of years ago."

He took me to the stasis bunker to show me how it all worked.

"You're a big boy now, and if anything should happen to me and your mother, or if we're not here, you need to be man enough to take control. Do you understand?"

"Yes, Dad," I said nodding.

"Good Lad. First you need to close the bunker door. After the door is shut, you need to put the bunker out of phase. Phasing will protect the structure against everything except a direct hit from a warhead, and that isn't likely out here in the sticks. Only major cities will be targeted."

"But, you will be here, Dad, won't you?"

"Of course, this is just in case I'm not. To put the bunker out of phase, enter the code. 19042099. Your sister's birthday. Okay?"

"19042099," I repeated.

"Then you're going to need to put the sleep capsules into stasis mode. Make sure your sister is in her capsule first, and that the lid is correctly shut, like so," he said, demonstrating how the lid lowered to create an airtight seal, "and simply enter the code again. Then press stasis. The countdown timer will start. One hundred years should be enough to give the radiation and fallout time to clear and for nature to take over again.

"If there is a malfunction, the stasis pod will come out of stasis early and you or your sister will be able to release the lid from the inside. If you wake early, you have to make a decision as to whether to release your sister too. Pay attention to the read out, at least fifty years has to have passed for the environment to be even tolerably safe. If less time than that has passed, then I would suggest—and this will be very difficult for you—I suggest you leave and try to make a life for yourself elsewhere.

"The more time that has passed between the bombs falling, and you or your sister's emergence into the world, the more chance you will have to survive.”

“What will it be like?” I asked.

“Don’t interrupt!” he snapped. Then he wiped his forehead with the sleeve of his shirt and continued. “Sorry, Pete, just pay attention. This pod, that we tested on Timmy and the one opposite are both working. The other two closest to the entrance are beyond my abilities to repair. I’ve arranged for a specialist, but it will be weeks before he can do the job. In the meantime, we must double up, but if your mum and me aren’t here, then take one capsule each.”

“But, you will be here,” I said.

“Just get to the bunker as quick as you can. Phase it, and when you’re ready, go into stasis.”

"But you will be here, won't you?"

I was desperate for reassurance that we wouldn't be left alone. I couldn't believe the things he was saying and it only got worse.

"If you and your sister are to survive, you'll need protection. This is an old stun laser; it's the best I could get. Don't dick around with it. It will send thirty thousand watts at a target."

He attached the laser to a charger in the far wall. That end of the bunker had lots of storage cabinets with tinned and dried food. Then he drew a thin, sharp knife from one of the drawers.

"This is an old knife that used to belong to one of your ancestors. He was in the army I think. Your great-grandfather always kept it in great condition. It slit the throat of a great German called Nazi once. All I really know is that this might save your life one day, so take care of it. And this one is for your sister, it's a little ankle knife. Strap it to her leg before you send her into stasis. Do you understand?"

"Yes, Dad."

"I hope the longer we're in stasis, the less need there will be for violence. In a world fragmented by war, many individuals will strive to gain the upper hand and take power. As time moves on, I hope society will stabilise. It will be easier to survive if we are not a part of that initial struggle. Do you understand?"

"Yes Dad, but—"

"I haven't finished, Pete. Do not trust

anyone. In a dangerous situation, the likes of which I have no idea of yet, trust must be earned. Do not give your food or your weapons to anyone. Always have them ready and do not be afraid to use them. Do you understand?"

"Yes, Dad."

"I don't think you do, Pete. You may arrive in a world where the survivors are so starved they'll eat other people."

"Dad, you're scaring me."

"Good. When you meet someone new, have your hand on the laser or the knife and be ready to kill."

"But, Dad."

"Right, that's it. One of the chickens needs slaughtering; you should have learnt to do this a long time ago. Let's go."

We had a chicken coup near the house. We weren't farmers or anything like that, just a bit green. We had a vegetable patch too, growing carrots and parsnips. He reached into the coup and, after a bit of feather flying and squawking, pulled a chicken out, its wings flapping like crazy.

"Of course, the traditional way to kill a chicken is simply to twist its neck, but I want you to get used to using that knife to kill. It's what it was designed for. So go on, cut the bird's head off."

"But, Dad, what good's a knife against lasers and god knows what sort of guns will be around in a hundred years."

"When those bombs start falling nothing survives. Nothing, Pete. Buildings are flattened, metal is melted, people vanish in the blink of an eye and mountains tumble as if they never existed. Only something out of phase will have a chance of surviving. I'm going to find everything I can that might be useful and store it in the bunker. Your great uncle Jim might have old shooting guns he could give us.

"Now, kill the bloody chicken."

His red eyes told me how upsetting he found all this. His hands shook as he held the chicken out for me to slaughter. I thought he might have gone insane as I stepped forward and raised the blade. The chicken had calmed down a little, perhaps accepting its fate. I tried to steady my hand as I touched the sharp edge of the knife to its throat.

"Do I have to, Dad?"

"Do it," he snapped.

So I did it, warm blood spurting on to my face and hands. As I ran back to the house crying, I heard Mum shouting at Dad. I puked into the toilet bowl. It took hours to wash the blood off.

Later that day, I saw my dad plucking the bird.

"He means well; he's just worried about us," Mum said later, "and I'm worried about him. I'll try to get him to see a doctor tomorrow. I'm so sorry he made you do that, Pete. Are you okay?"

Lying on my bed, with my back to her, I couldn't think of anything to say. She left me to my uneasy sleep.

***

The next day the sirens went off. The inweb in my head became so loud with the noise, I thought I might faint. My sister and I were alone in the house, as my father was at the doctor's with my mother. I had to carry my sister to the bunker—her inweb safety protocols had malfunctioned—she must have been in agony. Timmy trotted along next to us, his normal exuberant self somewhat deflated. I think he knew what was happening. The world was about to burn.

I locked the door, phased the bunker, and settled down to wait for my parents. The viewing portal gave me a view down to our house. The minutes ticked by, and then they came bursting through the back door, Dad dragging Mum by the hand. She had lost a shoe. I could see him yelling at her to run faster. But, the garden must have been a hundred feet long. My finger floated over the open button for the bunker door. I knew I would have to wait till the last minute before I let them in. Even then if the timing were wrong, I might not have time to phase the bunker again.

Half way along the garden, Dad slipped and fell. Mum was trying to lift him. She was trying to drag him to his feet, but he froze, and my mum followed his gaze to the sky. She stopped trying, and simply knelt with him. Each of them hanging to the other so tightly. She crossed herself, and I could see her lips moving as she said a prayer.

Then everything went white.

Less than two minutes later I could see again, and I wish to God I hadn't looked. Everything was gone, our house, our garden, our parents, were just gone. The ground bled red and boiling blood. The heavens looked like a living bruise. The sky, dark green with purple and black clouds, moving so fast it looked like time had been sped up.

I was too shocked to do anything but watch. I had never known silence like it. Sound could not penetrate the bunker and the inweb was gone. Nothing was there. No messages, no news updates, no recordings of family events. The images of our entire family all the way back to the turn of the twenty-first century were simply gone, as if they had never existed.

No one could ever feel as alone as I did then. Eventually, I went back to Joanne, whom I had laid in one of the stasis chambers. She was still unconscious. Timmy lay alongside her, he looked up at me, his big eyes looking sadder than ever, and I knew he knew what had happened. I found the knife my dad had said to strap to her leg and I did as instructed. Timmy licked my hand and I stroked his ears. Then I lowered the chamber door and entered the code. The display began its countdown:

Years	days	hours	mins	secs
99	364	23	59	59

I took my own knife to my chamber in case I needed it the minute I came to, lay down, and activated the stasis with a press of a button.

And then I lowered my hand. I thought, *Oh God, it's not working, and I'm gonna die in here 'cause I sure as shit can't go out into that hell beyond the viewer.*

I nearly entered the code again, but something felt strange. I looked over at Joanne's chamber only to see the lid up. It gave me such a start that I sat upright and hit my head on the chamber door. I fumbled for the release mechanism and staggered over to her pod. She was gone, as was Timmy.

The countdown clock said she had twenty five years left in hibernation. It must have malfunctioned and released her early. My own clock read zero. This was so strange; one hundred years had passed for me in the blink of an eye.

Some empty tins lay strewn on the worktop, rodents having striped them clean long ago. A faded note from Joanne was pinned under one of the tins.

Der Pety
Me and Timmy hav to go now
Luv Joany

If I thought I was alone earlier, I was mistaken.

The door was open and sunlight poured through. I cautiously stepped out onto lush green grass. A cherry tree grew in the middle of what should have been our garden, in the place I imagined where our parents had knelt. I decided that I must find my sister. I didn't know how, or where, but I had to try. She had to be somewhere, didn't she?

If she had lived, she would be about thirty-five years old. My little sister would be older than me. She might even have children of her own.

I started walking.

**First published in *World War Four,*
Zombie Pirate Publishing, 2019**

THE IRONY OF PROSPERINE

By Galina Trefil

"Max out the credit cards," Ben murmured softly against Hannah's ear as they entered the Wal-Mart Supercenter. "Use every last cent. When your cart is full, call me. I'll load up the supplies. In the meantime, I'll empty the savings and checking accounts. When the U-Haul can't fit any more, I'll drive back to the property and switch vehicles."

"How many times are we going to have to do this?"

"Until the money's gone." His dark eyebrows knit, and staring straight ahead, he seemed somewhat absent from her suddenly. But that was to be expected, given that he had killed someone three hours ago.

She glanced down at his hand, swallowing, and gave it a gentle, reassuring squeeze. "You know that you did what you had to. You have no reason to feel guilty."

Ben's eyelids drooped halfway closed. "You seriously think I care about him dying? I don't. I wanted to kill him ever since I found out about him. This just gave me the excuse and the opportunity."

"Then what?"

"I just thought there might be some kind of call to evacuate by now, but…"

The two of them looked out at the bustling crowd before them. At the checkout stands, tired parents tried to keep their kids from throwing tantrums over toys and candy. Gangs of teenagers walked together down aisles, gossiping about celebrities, crushes, and fashion trends. A pair of young, giggling lovers stopped to look through the jewelry section at the engagement rings. And while their bored husbands killed time at the in-store Subway, ladies pampered themselves with facials and manicures at a moderately-priced, adjoining beauty salon.

"They're all going to die," Ben

whispered. "And they have no idea…"

"It's better this way," Hannah stated softly. "There's not enough time to evacuate. And there's nowhere to go. We'll probably die right along with them."

That comment brought her husband away from his inner turmoil like the crack of a whip. "No," he declared firmly, placing his palms against her cheeks and giving her a brief but determined kiss. "We're going to survive. You, me, and the others…we'll live. For a few years at least. Until the supplies run dry. And it's all because of you."

Now it was her forehead creasing with distress. No matter what Ben said, she knew that their lives wouldn't be spared because of her. Instead, it was all thanks to a rich, old bastard who was now lying mutilated in a puddle of his own blood.

"We don't have time for this," Hannah replied evasively. "I'll call you when I'm ready to load up."

They went their separate ways. As she began to ransack the canned goods and other storage-friendly food in the grocery store, she fought unsuccessfully to keep the memories of her youth from overwhelming her.

Fourteen years old. Cleaning houses in order to pay for college. Saving up to buy herself a way out of life in the projects, where cockroaches nested in the ceiling and occasionally fell down into her hair…and, with its locale being right next to the red light district, the outside was even worse.

As an adult, in retrospect, Hannah could admit that it would have been only been a matter of time before one of her employers tried to take advantage of her, the girl from the wrong side of the tracks, in one way or another. Everyone knew her parents were drug addicts who wouldn't protect her. Hell, they were so high that they didn't even notice for three days that she hadn't come home.

"Well, well, girlie, look what you've gone and done," Mr. Whitney's voice had cracked as she stood there in short braids, vacuum still in one hand, gaping down at the hole in his closet. "You know that I'm just going to have to keep you now, don't you? That's what you get for not staying out of this room as I instructed you to."

"I won't tell anybody, sir," she'd choked. "I don't even know what it is. I didn't look inside it, I swear."

The middle-aged man had grabbed her skinny frame up in the air as if she were nothing but a toothpick. Then he'd dragged her to the hole and started to shove her underground. She'd fought, but ultimately lost. Fortunately, she was able to grab the metal bars leading downward to keep from falling to the cement floor far below. Before she had a chance to scream for help, he'd slammed the metal frame above her head closed. To this day, she still awoke crying, recalling the sound of the bolt locking shut.

Sometimes she found herself sitting

over coffee, not believing that any of it had ever happened at all. And sometimes she felt as though she had never escaped; that she was still in the secret bunker, imagining what kind of life she would have if she one day broke free.

Terribly ironic that, after spending a year in that dungeon, wishing that she could only get away, now she was complicit in the brutally executed murder of her former captor for the sole purpose of getting back inside. Ironic as well that, if not for her imprisonment, she would be like all the people shopping around her—fated for imminent death. Only, unlike them, she would not be carefree. No, indeed, because she knew what was coming. And there were a total of eight men, six women, and nine children enthusiastically going into that cage to get away from the impending destruction.

Whitney, a through-and-through survivalist, had long planned for the end of the world. According to what he'd repeatedly told her, it was only a matter of time before the Cold War—which had, of course, never truly resolved—grew white-hot. He'd claimed that he had enough water, dehydrated food, and other supplies in the bunker where he'd held her captive to last for two and a half decades. Courtesy of him being a multi-millionaire several times over, the bunker, as Hannah remembered it, was designed not for personal use, but for the subterranean housing of up to one hundred military men.

Three connected columns ran roughly the length of a football field. There was a recreation area, an infirmary, storage facility, and while simple soldiers had small beds which pulled down from the walls in their crowded barrack area, there was a separate bedroom entirely for only the commander's use.

Hair on the back of her neck prickling, she shuddered. He'd called that place "The Underworld." He'd called her, for good measure, "Eurydice." He'd probably been planning on keeping her down there from the first time that she naively rang his doorbell, holding out her little homemade flier discussing her hourly rates and what times after school she was available to work. Why else, after all, would a guy that rich hire a kid?

Hannah realised that she was squeezing the handlebar of the shopping cart so hard that her knuckles were turning white.

When Ben had asked, Whitney hadn't been willing to give up the combination to the lock to get inside the bunker. Even tied up and beaten, he wouldn't initially reveal the numbers. Good. She was glad he'd stubbornly forced the interrogation to go to a whole new level of violent. An eye for an eye may have been delayed, but, after fifteen years, it had finally come due.

The only reason that she had ever gotten out at all was because, when he'd come down to "visit" her one day, he'd been too drunk to remember to lock the hatch behind him. When he'd passed out, she'd escaped, and upon arriving home, she found out that her parents, as well as the police, had simply assumed her to be a runaway. The search for her had ranged somewhere between minimal and non-existent. When she explained everything that had happened to her, her parents had been more interested in bleeding Whitney's bank account than ensuring he go to prison. In the end, a private sum was settled on. They managed to go through half of it before they overdosed on the drugs that it had bought them.

Years later, the remaining blood money sent Hannah to a top-notch university, where she invented a new background for herself and pretended that her entire life before was nothing but a terrible nightmare. She excelled in her studies, graduated, and wound up working for NASA at the Goldstone Observatory in the Mojave Desert. She'd met Ben there and several of the other scientists who were out now doing their "last minute shopping."

Standing near the pharmacy, the full weight of the situation crushed her. How did a person possibly fathom this anyway, she wondered? How did you decide which items to pull off the shelves, knowing that if you forgot anything, it would quite possibly be the last time in your life that you would encounter that item again? This was the last day that she would ever see the little frivolities that humans had come to take for granted, like teddy bears, scented candles, and mascara. But the true luxuries like shampoo, tampons, aspirin—heck, quality shoes and socks—what was life going to be like without any access to them? And, if she and her group did survive the next few days, only to endure the hell of the upcoming years, what things was she looking at now that she would curse herself later for not buying?

It was the sort of question that, if she were a paranoid lunatic like her former captor, would have been easy to answer. But she wasn't. She bought cart after cart of items, many more of them random than she knew was wise. The U-Haul gradually filled. An empty one took its place. She knew that her co-workers and their immediate families were all working themselves to the bone, foraging just the same as her. But, by nightfall, their eagerness had taken on a different tune. Their eyes drifted increasingly towards the sky and, even though they knew there was still time, they dreaded each trip away from the bunker more and more. Math and logic, when it came to the space, had a way of being relative at the least opportune moments, as they had learned all too harshly within the last forty-eight hours.

It was truly some kind of a beautiful bitch that was to be their undoing. Named Proserpine, she had fled her orbit inside the asteroid belt to head close to earth, coming in at a speed of over twenty-two thousand miles per hour. They'd all been aware of her for years. At three miles across, the rock sphere filled with hydrogen, carbon, and oxygen was hard to miss. There had been a great deal of talk recently amongst astronomers about the possibility of mining asteroids, and Proserpine had been considered, with her vast amount of frozen water, platinum, and gold, a strong potential candidate for such endeavours in the future. She circled near Earth—near enough for her to look good to miners—but, especially after the Chelyabinsk meteor hit in 2013, injuring well over a thousand people in remote Siberia, Proserpine was always watched to ensure that "near" did not mean "near enough" for an actual collision.

"We could have destroyed her,"

Kathy, a NASA mathematician, told Hannah later that evening when the shopping was over. On the front lawn of Whitney's mansion, the two of them took one long last look up at the stars. "You know that, don't you? All of those people that are going to die, they didn't know that she even existed. But we did. And we let her stay there, coiling around us like a snake, and didn't do anything. We don't deserve to be the ones who survive this."

"None of this has anything to do with what people deserve."

"We are five hundred miles from the predicted place of impact," Kathy replied, her tone taking on more of a growl with each passing word. "Once Proserpine comes into Earth's gravitational pull, it will only take her four minutes to speed up to forty-five thousand miles per hour. The friction of that will turn the rock into a thirty-five thousand degree fireball and, when that fireball hits, all the townspeople here will be able to see the light from it because its brightness will stretch up to one eighth around the world. Seconds later, for all the distance between us and ground zero, temperatures here will reach six hundred degrees and that will burn the eyes right out of the heads of every person that we saw today. The liquid in their bodies will evaporate and explode through their skin."

She glared at Hannah coldly. "Do not downplay our accountability. Our entire species may not survive because we were careless. We spent money on wars, on politics, on feeding corporations, when the thing which could wipe us out in the blink of an eye was right under our noses the entire time. We had the technology to cause Proserpine to break apart when it was still far enough away. We had the technology to knock it far off into a different orbit. And we could have had the proper technology to keep an eye on smaller asteroids, even when they were coming from our blind spot, but we didn't do it. We didn't invest fast enough—not the money and not the man-hours. Chelyabinsk was a warning and we didn't pay attention. We were too busy with other things. And that will wind up killing us, killing everything."

Kathy rubbed at her moistened eyes.

"Did you know that I really love tomatoes? When we talk about the meteor that killed the dinosaurs, we never mention how much of the vegetation died with them, either because it was burned up or because of the acid rains that followed. And today, when we were shopping, I walked through the produce aisle and wondered, 'Will I ever see tomatoes again?' I mean, here I am, with little kids who are about to die horribly on all sides of me, and what do I do? I go to the gardening section and grab tomato seeds. I get all kinds of seeds and pots and fertiliser. Everything that I can think of which might create food, trees, and flowers again after we eventually come back out of that bunker. Because everything that we're looking at now, down to every last blade of grass, is going to be gone, burned up by a fifteen-thousand degree ejecta cloud that's going to spread out at least two thousand miles in all directions from ground zero—quite possibly three thousand. But, even if not for the ejecta cloud, the dust that will go into the air after the asteroid's impact will cover the earth for years, blocking out the sun's light… So photosynthesis might not even be possible and my getting all these seeds might just have been useless. Meanwhile, maybe I could have saved just one child…and I didn't. I have to live with that. You tell me how I live with that, Hannah, because I don't know."

"The dinosaurs were wiped out by an asteroid twice Proserpine's size.

Depending on the angle that she hits at, things might not be nearly so bad."

"The moon still has a fifty-mile crater on it from an asteroid Proserpine's size crashing into it. Don't patronise me about what's going to happen. I was here…standing by while that old man screamed and pleaded for his life…not interfering, letting the violence happen…because I knew that it was the only way that we were going to survive what's about to occur. And that too, I have to live with."

"No," Hannah murmured. "No, you don't."

"Oh? And why is that?"

"Because I would rather have the eyes burned from my head than see him, of all people, live through this."

"None of us are in a position to judge the wrong-doings of others, Hannah," Kathy scowled, storming away. "Not anymore."

As Hannah walked inside Whitney's house, she tried to brush aside her nausea, but she still threw up. With all the commotion of people rushing back and forth, carrying things from their shopping runs as well as personal items and things plundered from the estate down into the hole, no one even took notice as she leaned one hand against the wall to puke. There had already been too many hysterics, emotional and physical, for one more event to make a difference.

Ben found her staggering, wiping at

the vomit that dribbled off her chin. "Have you been down there yet?" she inquired, repressing the urge to upchuck again.

"Yes."

"And did you find any things…" She looked down at the floor, trying to find a way to phrase it. "Things that deserve to be incinerated?"

"Yes. They were right where you said that they'd be. I carried them outside. No one saw me." He put a soothing hand on her shoulder and then wiped her skin clean with the cuff of his sleeve. "None of the pictures were of you anyway. He probably got rid of all that back when you escaped, just in case the cops caught him."

"Kathy is going to be confrontational. I almost said something, but—"

"You won't have to."

"Why not? We butchered him. Bad enough in her mind you and I were involved, but her own husband joined in… She'll never let that go. She'll hate us both for that, but me especially."

"I don't think so."

"Why not?"

"Because he had someone down there again. Another girl."

Hannah's eyes went wide. "What?"

Ben tucked the hair behind her ears gently. "You know how men like that are. They never do it just once."

Hannah lost her balance, but he grabbed her, holding her up. "How long has she been down there?"

"Forever."

"How long, Ben?" Hannah shrieked.

"Her entire life. She was born there. She's never been out, never even seen a photograph of what it looks like beyond the bunker. She thinks Whitney is God, above-ground is Heaven, and that where he kept her is the real world."

"Jesus," she whispered. "What did that fundamentalist nutjob name her anyway? Eve?"

"No," Ben sighed hesitantly. "He named her Hannah."

At these words, she slumped forward in speechless misery. Ben held her, running his hand over her back. "As for the mother, she was—the little girl says—called Eve. She died down there and Whitney carried her body out. Who knows what he did with the body or who she really was."

"He was just going to keep her down there until the end of time, wasn't he?"

"Well, in a way, he did. If this wasn't likely about to be the end of recorded time, she would never have been found."

"And all it took was a three-mile-long asteroid being knocked out of its safe orbit by the impact of a much smaller rogue asteroid which our telescope never detected until it was too late."

"What were the chances?" Ben murmured the question which couldn't stop running through all of their heads.

"If Rogue just hadn't come from the direction of the sun, we'd have seen it. We'd have made sure that it couldn't hit Proserpine."

"And then Proserpine couldn't hit us…"

"If we'd only had the space telescope launched just a bit sooner, it would have detected Rogue, no matter where it came from, but…"

"There's too many 'if onlys.' There's nothing that we can do about it now."

She leaned away from him and looked him dead in the eyes. "All this effort…this preparation…might very well be for nothing. The impact from Proserpine is going to send seismic waves across the planet that will set off the biggest earthquakes mankind has ever experienced. The dinosaurs that didn't die automatically still had to undergo…what was the number?"

"An 11.1 on the Richter scale."

"The worst earthquake that we know humans have ever gone through was only 9.6. What's coming is over fifty times worse. That entire bunker could collapse from the strain."

"Or the fact that it is underground will preserve us from the heat of the fireball. That's the only reason small mammals didn't go extinct when dinosaurs did. There's no use being pessimistic, Hannah. This is our best chance. Hell, this is our only chance."

She held her slender fist against her mouth, biting at the knuckle of her pointer finger for a moment. "I don't know how to go back down into the underworld, Ben. I don't know if I can do it. I know that's the dumbest thing ever to say right now. I thought that I would be tougher, but now that the moment has arrived, I don't—"

"You *can,*" he told her solidly. "Of course, you can, Hannah. Let's ignore the fact for a second that I'm not going to let you stay up here and die. Just tell me this— who else but you is really going to be able to understand that little girl down there?"

She blinked, parted her lips to respond, and then only nodded.

Ben escorted her down slowly, very, *very* slowly, into the bunker. She had to admit, when she finally took in the surroundings, Whitney had changed it a great deal. It had been painted in some places, wall-papered in others. Comfy furniture and other "homey" odds and ends had been brought down, stripping it of its militaristic atmosphere. "It wasn't like this before," she stated anxiously. "It was cold, black, bleak. Awful."

"Why don't you come meet Hannah, Hannah," he suggested, trying to get her mind away from the interior's history.

The little girl looked just like Whitney, allowing no doubt that he was indeed her father. Despite having next to no other human contact for the entirety of her life, the child was remarkably friendly. "What's your name?" she asked, seeing the new face standing in front of her.

"The same as yours," adult Hannah choked.

"It's Hannah?" The ten-year-old's voice was incredulous as the adult nodded.

"Are you…the Other Hannah? The one who became Eurydice, the first wife of God?"

Adult Hannah shifted on her feet, feeling dizzy.

"Oh, you are, aren't you? I know all about you! You defied God. You forsook his laws."

"He wasn't God," adult Hannah quavered. "He was a monster."

The little girl looked at the ground matter-of-factly. "God used to tell me that He would die someday and, when He did, the world would die with Him. He told me that there would be a great starvation and thirst, followed eventually by total darkness. Is that why you've come back?"

Adult Hannah didn't respond. She

couldn't.

"Are you scared?" the little girl whispered, walking towards her. "You shouldn't be, you know. Death isn't anything but a natural change.

"God used to tell me that you didn't know how to live in the real world. He said that you wanted to go to Heaven so much that you didn't appreciate what you had. He named me after you, he said, so that I would learn from your mistake and accept a simple life, down here, where I belong."

She reached out and took Hannah's hand. "If the world is ending, I'm glad that you came home. I can teach you how to accept being here for the time that we have left. This isn't the bad place that you think it is. You can be happy. You and all your friends, we can all be happy."

"Guys!" They heard Kathy scream from outside. "Proserpine's meteor shower is starting! Everybody get down in the hole fast!"

Amidst others' screams, prayers, and sobs, Hannah pulled her hand away from the child and sank down on a nearby couch. Ben wrapped his arms around her, as if bracing for the impact.

Proserpine—the Roman term for Eurydice. Was the name just another in a long string of ironies? Perhaps the asteroid was a kindred spirit, for both it and Hannah had certainly returned, in blood and carnage, to claim the underworld as their own.

What would happen from here on out

was only God's guess, but He was no longer talking.

Mother Nature had the microphone now. And she had one hell of a mouthful to say.

**First published in *Suspense Unimagined*,
Left Hand Publishers, 2019**

CAMPFIRE SONGS

By Kimberly Rei

The woods grew darker as the sun slipped behind the horizon. It meant that maybe the howling band that chased me would drift off in search of easier prey. But it also meant howling creatures of another kind were just starting to stir. Everything was howling and hungry these days, it seemed. There was a good chance I had sealed my fate by running past the treeline, but I'd rather take my chances with wolves. They only ate your flesh.

I kept moving in the hope of finding something I could set my back against. An empty cave would be perfect, but a tight crop of trees might work. I had learned as a child how to move swiftly over just about any terrain, so I dodged roots and bushes with ease. A patch of slick mud nearly took me down, and I slammed a shoulder into a large trunk. I'd feel that later.

A fresh howl broke out behind me, far too close for comfort, and sent me pounding over roots and leaves once more, a fresh burst of terror giving me speed. I glanced over my throbbing shoulder, and when I turned back, the trees had opened to a clearing. Voices. I heard someone talking! They didn't seem to care who heard them. Were they fools? Moving too fast to skid to a halt, I braced myself for the burst of pain that came with a drop-and-roll behind a rusted out car. The distant voices drew closer. I couldn't let myself be seen. Not until I knew who they were. What they were. My gaze flicked around, frantic. This car wouldn't hide me for long.

A neat row of decrepit houses stood a good dash away. They'd been bombed and looted, but one near the middle seemed to have survived. Most of the windows were unbroken. The front door hung by one hinge, which was a hinge more than the others. The house stood at least three floors high, with what looked like an attic. There was a chance it was inhabited, but if so, no one was moving around inside.

The voices grew louder. It was now or never. My shoulder twinged as I pushed off the rusty beast and ran, dust kicking up behind me. There was no help for that. I could only hope the people coming this way would not notice my footprints. Checking my pace, I ducked through the door and pressed against the first wall I found. It is a skill to keep from panting when you are scared and desperate for breath. You must breathe in slowly through your nose, out gently through your mouth. Slow the heart rate and breathing. Remain silent. Listen.

Nothing. Could this place truly be abandoned? Or were the inhabitants returning home even now?

As quickly and carefully as I knew how, I ran up the stairs. All of them. I didn't stop until I reached a solid-looking door at the top. The layer of dust on the handle said it hadn't been used in years. If anyone came after me, one glance at that knob and the smeared dirt would give me away. Still, it was a chance I had to take if I wanted to hide, even for a night. No sane soul dared go unsheltered at night.

Dim light came through the window as I opened the door, then closed it behind me. My eyes widened in wonder. Was that a bed? A real bed? It was small, as if meant for a child, but not so small that I couldn't rest there. A dresser. A smaller desk with a great big mirror attached and a cushioned seat nearby. Shelf after shelf graced the walls, filled with toys. It was as if the war and destruction had left this room entirely alone. As if the fallout didn't matter, the bands of desperate people didn't exist. As if I had stepped into a place forgotten by truth.

I sat on the bed and nearly wept. It would take a day or two, maybe more, to be sure this house wasn't taken. But if my luck held out, I might have a new home!

A full moon rose slowly, glowing as red as ever, but for the first time in a long time, I was not afraid. I was too intrigued. I no longer heard the voices and there seemed to be no movement at all in the house, so I wandered the room freely, picking up various objects and turning them over in my hand. The hairbrush didn't do much for my short tangle, but it was still fun to use. After all, I hadn't seen one in more than a decade. A delicate beaded bracelet fell apart in my hands when I picked it up, scattering tiny bits of colour across the wood floor and into the throw rugs. I trailed my fingers over the shelves, marvelling that they still hung so straight and strong.

And that's when I saw her. A pretty little doll, the size of a newborn babe. She was wearing a blue and white checked dress and little blue shoes. There was even lace on her white socks. How had they stayed so clean? I was afraid to touch her and make her dirty, but her blonde hair looked so soft, I couldn't resist. I picked her up carefully and stroked that hair, playing with the curls. She was beautiful enough to move me to tears.

As I ran my fingers through the silken yellow, one caught on a plastic ring and I tried to yank my hand away. A cheerful voice filled the room, "Hello! I'm Cathy! What's *your* name?"

I almost dropped her. What trickery was this? Was she a spy's tool? A radio? Was there a camera in those little eyes? I shook her. I turned her over and over, looking for proof. Nothing.

My name. What was my name? I hadn't thought of myself by a name in a very long time. And what if I answered her? Would she respond? I nibbled my cracked lip and took a chance, "I'm...I'm Sura. It's nice to meet you, Cathy."

Again, nothing. No response. If she was a plant, she was a sneaky one. Or maybe whoever had set her up had long since left their post. What if she was meant to help? She might have clues about this place.

I pulled the string again.

"Please take me with you."

I wasn't expecting that. Not the words or the shift in tone. The cheerfulness was gone, replaced by need. The hairs on the back of my neck started to rise. In any other circumstance, I would have listened and gotten out of there. But I needed to know more before I left this potential haven.

I pulled the string again. The doll shuddered in my hands. "Run, Sura. Run NOW!"

I ran. Down the stairs and out the front door, for once not caring who heard me. Survival instinct of a more primal nature took over. It wasn't until I was halfway between the rusted out car and the treeline that I paused for a breath.

That was when I noticed the doll was still in my hands. I nearly threw her from me, but something made my hand tighten instead. More of that instinct. I turned to look at the house and dropped to my knees, cradling Cathy against me. Red eyes blinked from the top window. One pair. Then another. More and more until the glass was nearly full of crimson winking on and off. I'd never seen anything like it, but Cathy had lived with it. Them. I knew then that she had saved me. Leaving her behind wasn't going to be an option.

I shifted, holding her a little more gracefully. Night had fallen, leaving only red moonglow. It didn't look like the eyes were planning to come after us. That left other, more immediate concerns to tend. I hadn't slept rough since my childhood and I didn't want to dust those skills off now. Unfortunately, this was fairly new territory to me. I'd been through once or twice before, but never long enough to get a good feel for the lay of the land. The loss of the house still stung and oddly clouded my ability to consider other options. I wanted to go back and stretch out in that clean bed. More than anything, I wanted to recapture that fleeting sensation that everything was going to be okay. The truth threatened to drag me down and under.

On a whim, I tugged the doll's cord. "Well? You got any bright ideas?"

"Auntie."

My grip tightened, and I stared into her glass eyes, "What did you say?"

Silence. I cursed whoever designed this puzzle and pulled the string, harder this time, as if that might power her for more than one answer.

"Ow! Auntie. We must find Auntie."

My head filled with a tumble of questions, but there wasn't time to ask any of them. The only idea worse than finding Auntie was staying out here much longer. The moon was reaching its peak, bringing with it the kind of night life best avoided. The howling started up again, far behind us. Not far enough if I could still hear it.

"Auntie. Tiny gods, doll, you do ask a lot."

I tucked her under my arm and took off at a ground-eating lope, leaning forward just enough to let my weight give me speed. It was an old trick, and it left you more tired at the end of the journey, but it helped ensure you'd arrive at all. My people had learned many ways to survive. A few had even been passed down to me.

Getting to Auntie wasn't the problem. Her lair was well known, at the centre of one of the permanent camps. A small town running on theft and barter had sprung up around her, paying homage in both cash and respect. No one knew where Auntie came from, but we all knew her role, even when we didn't know our own. Getting in to see her was the real trouble. Especially for me.

"You. You're banned, waif."

I wheezed, gasping for air. The run had taken more out of me than expected.

The rather large man blocking the doorway chuckled, "Best go back the way you came before she catches your scent. You remember what she said about seeing your face again?"

I nodded. I wasn't likely to forget so creative a death threat. One final wheeze and my voice crept back into my throat, "I have to risk it, Merry."

He chortled and shook his head, then stepped aside, "There might be enough left of you to keep the shades from our door tonight. Got anything of worth I should strip from your corpse?"

I ignored him and stepped into the maze of tents. In most places, the cloth rose high enough to stand upright, but now and then, I had to duck as I moved through the darkness. Muscle memory carried me to Auntie's chamber. The delicate lick of incense rewarded my instinct and turned my stomach. This was going to be rough.

I moved out of darkness and into flickering light. There were enough candles in this cloth suite to read by. More than enough for Auntie to recognise me the instant I entered the room. I blinked, pretending light blindness and trying to buy myself a moment.

Auntie sat on a raised dais, lounging

against a pile of silk and velvet pillows. There were enough to craft an impressive and cosy throne perched high to let long legs stretch and give her the air of a ruler. She was as close to royalty as the deadlands dared claim. I glanced at her, brushing my gaze quickly to drink in her mood. People lived and died by what Auntie was wearing on any given day. My stomach clenched.

Those long legs were encased in loose black pants that tightened as they climbed her form until they hugged high on her waist and gave way to a shirt more white than it had any right to be. It was a mystery of the lands, how she managed to keep anything so pristine. I had a flash of the lace on the doll's socks. That same white. Auntie's pleated shirt vanished into a flowing black jacket with darted sleeves spilling over the wildly coloured pillows. An ominous claret scarf hung around her neck.

I dared look up.

A top hat of respectable splendour rested on a waterfall of midnight blue hair. Had it been any other time, I would have clapped at the sight of such a perfect appearance. She looked phenomenal. Of course, I was ignoring the reason she wanted my head on a pike.

Auntie's voice flowed toward me, the tone deep and masculine and knotted with menace, "I never took you for a Fool, waif. Daring, perhaps, but never foolish."

Her voice froze what was left of hope. Auntie managed her world by never settling into one of anything. She was never entirely she, nor entirely he, though always She if you knew what was good for you. Only a cherished few knew exactly what lay beneath her elaborate costumes. As a gift to all of us, she used her appearance and persona as a warning of her moods. It would seem she had known I was coming. I wondered what method Merry used to inform her so swiftly.

She raised a filigree silver talon and stroked over the vicious scar that lived where an eye should. Puckered flesh was cut through with a red line that never seemed to lose its angry glow. I winced.

"Gives me a roguish air, does it not? Should I thank you, waif?"

"No, Auntie."

"Ah! It speaks. Then perhaps it can explain why it hauled its infernal hide back into my presence?"

The pattern of her words never shifted, but I could hear the fury in each casual syllable. I wanted to throw myself at her feet and beg her forgiveness. But if it hadn't worked when I accidentally took her eye, it certainly wouldn't work now.

"I found something of interest."

The silence stretched. She stared at me as if I had lost my mind. Nothing shy of another apocalypse should have brought me to her door and here I was, seemingly offering a tinker's bobble.

She shifted and held out a hand. I eased forward and gave her the doll. Her voice rose several octaves as she gently took my prize. She cradled it to her chest and leaned back, eyes closed against powerful emotion, "Where did you find this?"

"In an abandoned house. The room at the very top. It was perfect, Auntie! I swear, time forgot to pass there."

"Yes. It would. By the tiny gods, how did you manage to bring her to me?"

I shook my head, confused. "I just picked her up."

"Did she speak to you?"

"She told me to run."

Auntie rose and stepped down to glare at me. She was taller than I remembered. Or maybe I just felt terribly small.

"How? She only speaks to *yetemeret'u.*"

"The Chosen? Auntie! Is that...am

I...am..." My voice stuck as the weight of that one word settled on my shoulders.

Auntie burst into laughter, the sound sinking into the cloth tent walls, "No, idiot. *Yetemeret'u* was born eight cycles ago. This doll was her protector."

She folded herself onto the floor, legs crossed, and motioned for me to do the same. I obeyed, grateful I had seemingly done something right. I might survive this night after all. Merry was going to have to find another sacrifice for the shades.

"Guardian. What happened?" Auntie held the doll on her lap, looking into the blue glass eyes.

I reached for the plastic ring, "I had to pull this to make her talk."

The slap rang loud and carried a sharp

sting. I snatched my hand back, giving Auntie a wounded look.

"Foolish waif. Be silent and learn. Guardian. Will you speak with me?"

"Of course, Holy One."

I found a spot on the rug to stare at, deliberately not responding outwardly to the honorific. I could feel Auntie staring at me, waiting for me to chew on my foot. The moment stretched out. Finally, Auntie turned her attention back to the doll.

"What happened to the child? What happened to your defences?"

Cathy was silent for so long, I thought she'd shut down or was refusing to tell the tale. Her porcelain body shuddered and if she hadn't been a doll, I would have said she sagged in Auntie's grip. Her head lifted and she turned to stare at the blank cloth wall.

The wall transformed from tent to stone. A bright room stretched further and wider than the current space. The marble fountain happily burbling was the same pristine white as the floors and walls. Matching columns broke the space up into a bathing area, an open closet, a play room, and a bedroom with a massive, raised bed. I could swim in that fluffy comforter and sleep like the dead against the silk pillows piled high. A young girl sat in the middle of the bed, stark and gorgeous. She was almost too thin, but it made her look ethereal rather than scrawny. She wore a silk froth of a dress, just as white as the rest of the room. Her hair fell in equally pale waves, pooling around her. When she moved, there was an abalone shimmer to the strands. Her skin, though, was the most glorious deep ebony, drinking in the light and tossing it back gently. Leaf green eyes, bright and nearly mythic in shade, danced as she chattered away to Cathy.

A door to the right opened and several men burst into the room. They were covered head to toe in deep crimson cloth, only their eyes showing. The tallest grabbed the child and clamped a hand over her mouth. She thrashed and clawed at him, but he simply tucked her under his arm like a sack.

"Disable that thing!"

Another man aimed a hand at Cathy. His palm glowed, then flared with an overly-bright blue flash. The vision shivered and began to fade. Before it winked out completely, I hear the tall man snarl again, "Bring it along. It's more obvious left behind."

I started to ask what happened after that when the image returned. My words shifted on their way up my throat, "That's the room! That's where I found Cathy!"

Another slap, this time to the back of my head. But it was true. The same skinny bed, the same dresser, the same desk and mirror. And the same shelves. Both the child and the doll sat on the bed, but the girl wasn't chattering. She was staring out of the window, her leaf green eyes dull and saddened. I wanted to step into the scene and wrap her up in a warm embrace.

Cathy didn't look right, either. She wasn't speaking or moving at all. Her eyes were locked and vacant. Clearly she was recording, but whatever her other skills, she couldn't access them. She was as helpless to protect the child as I was.

I tensed as the door opened, quietly this time. The men had returned. My hands curled into fists and I willed myself to stay still and silent. There was nothing I could do but bear witness. And so I would, in every detail.

They wore the same crimson uniforms. Only the tall man stood out as different from the others. Both his height and body shape marked him, and I vowed I would never forget him. I had nowhere to go with my ferocity, but it would help keep me warm.

The tall man lifted the child again. She didn't fight this time. She hung limp when he tossed her over his shoulder.

"Straighten up in here. Make it look like it's been empty. Leave the doll. No one who finds it will know what it is. Damn thing will explode if we cause it too much harm. Last one took out two units."

He left with the child. His men smoothed the bed and tucked Cathy onto a shelf where she sat, still unmoving. Once again, the vision faded. Nothing followed.

Auntie straightened, "Well then. I don't suppose you learned anything while you sat there in limbo?"

Cathy chuckled and it was an odd sound. Part grating, part liquid, and part actual amusement. As if she had either been inhaling for years or had forgotten how to laugh.

"I did, actually. There are creatures hunting her. They came sniffing around after dark. I could not make out much more than red eyes."

I trembled.

Auntie nodded and rose, lifting the doll. She set Cathy on a table beside her pillow throne, "I don't know what those are, but I know your crimson-clad thieves. And I know what that bright flash was. I can protect you against it."

Cathy was silent and I had to bite my lip. All this was going far too slow. I wanted action. I wanted to save the child and be the hero! If I wasn't yetemeret'u, I could rescue her. They would sing songs of me around campfires and I would be welcome at every outpost. I sighed into the vision and earned another slap to the back of my head.

"You should be listening instead of dreaming, waif."

I didn't bother wondering how she knew. Auntie always knew. I refocused half-way through a sentence.

"…where we can find a former Kith. He may even know what the creatures are or where they came from. He's deep in hiding. No one leaves the Kith. But I have a chit I can call in. I assume you'll travel with my people to speak with him?"

"I would prefer to, yes."

My mouth got away from me, "I want

to go, too!"

I ducked just in time.

Auntie actually laughed, "You truly are a Fool. No, waif, you're going to the training camps."

My heart fluttered and hope, that thing I had been squashing for so many years, stirred in my ribs, "I am?"

Auntie smiled. She reached up to the horrible scar covering her missing eye. Guilt lashed at me again. Her filigree talon stroked the puckered flesh. She watched me for a long moment, silent, then slipped that talon under her skin and peeled it away. I clamped both hands over my mouth to smother a scream. Auntie laughed again, but kept pulling until the scarred, ugly, and apparently fake, flesh tore away. I was expecting to see blood and tissue and a gaping hole. Instead, her skin was smooth and perfect and both eyes blinked at me.

"You had the courage to come after me when you thought I had wronged you. You stood your ground when you thought you'd blinded me. Then you had the courage to come back, knowing the price you would pay. You have spirit, girl. If we can beat some sense into you, we might make some use of you. If you're willing, Merry will take you to the training camps and we'll see."

I wanted to argue and beg to accompany Cathy. I had found her, after all. Surely I had a right to see this through. What about the campfire songs? But sense rose to cover all the whining.

"Thank you, Auntie. I won't let you down."

And that, waifs, is how I came to be here. Now, what's your story?

First published in *Luna Station Quarterly Issued 34, 2018*

ABOUT THE PUBLISHER

BLACK HARE PRESS is a small, independent publisher based in Melbourne, Australia.

Founded in 2018, our aim has always been to champion emerging authors from all around the globe and offer opportunities for them to participate in speculative fiction and horror short story anthologies.

Connect

Website: *www.blackharepress.com*

Twitter: *@BlackHarePress*